DEDICATION

This book is for
Todd, Charlotte, Rebecca, and Jennifer

Author's Note

I can't say exactly when the characters in this story started whispering to me, but I do remember the day I decided to put their nonsense down on paper. It was after listening to Bill Wittliff, the legendary Texas writer, give one of his final author's talks. It was in early 2019, not many weeks before he died. I was at Chez Zee American Bistro in Austin, Texas, at an intimate gathering of locals, all of us starstruck as he wove behind-the-scenes tales about the making of *Lonesome Dove*.

I'm confident he'd told the stories dozens of times, but still they entertained because, after all, it was Bill. Then there came a moment when I felt he was saying what every author needs to hear. What I needed to hear. He was passing on wisdom from his mentor, J. Frank Dobie, through him, to me. Simple words that stuck with me and inspired me as I wrote this book.

He said authentic fiction is built on the stories of our lives. That simple truth resonated. I've been blessed in my life with people who have shared interesting, passionate, heartbreaking, funny stories with me. One of the advantages of being old, and there are damn few, is you've had a lifetime to collect precious stories. I drew from the well of my lived experience and the stories I've heard from others to give flesh and bone to the characters who populate my make-believe little Texas town. Dobie once said the story belongs to whoever can best tell it. I hope that proves true for the citizens of Lantz, because they are now the custodians of my lifetime collection of tall tales.

Thank you, Bill. May God rest your soul. Thank you, also, to the storytellers I've known who made my life a lot more fun.

WHO'S WHO

- **Sheriff Ray Crawford Osborne** – Narrator and storyteller.
- **Sweet Wife** [or "**S.W.**"] – Sheriff's spouse and reliable source of the latest town gossip.
- **Veda Isabella (Miss Belle) Tackett** – The victim. Unloved and feared by most folks in Lantz, she's middle-aged and losing her looks.
- **Blake Tackett** – Husband of the victim and prime suspect. Persnickety and quiet, he's one of the Three B's.
- **Miss Lilly Tackett** – Only child of the victim. In her mid-thirties, she's independent-minded and sharp-tonged.
- **Hattie Mae Cooper** – Longtime housekeeper at the Tackett place. Nothing much gets past her.
- **Sara (Lawrence) Evans** – Chief cook and bottle washer at Lantz General Store. She believes you don't get mad. You get even.
- **Grace Elizabeth (Beth) Lawrence** – Sara's ancient and infirm mother. She clutches her Bible close.
- **Twizy** [aka "Hell Cat"] – Sara's fifteen-pound Maine Coon. This feline terrorizes everyone.

- **Jonathan Francis (Buster) McCombs** – Asshole who descended into alcoholism when he returned from Vietnam. One of the Three B's.
- **Edward (Ed) McCombs** – Buster's nephew and Afghan combat veteran with wounds you can't see. He keeps company with Miss Lilly.
- **Robert Wayne (Bobby) Seville, Sr.** – Nicest guy in town but has a bone to pick with the victim. His easy smile covers a broken heart. One of the Three B's.
- **Monica Seville** – Bobby's late wife. Ashes in an urn and fond memories are all that are left.
- **Robert Wayne (R.W.) Seville, Jr.** – Bobby's son. Talking too much is his way of hiding secrets from others.
- **Katie Sue Brooks** – The indispensable dispatcher at the sheriff's office. Her conversation rambles but her computer skills are spot on.
- **Deputy Johnnie Lake** – Part-time deputy. He's often missing in action.
- **Phillip (Phil) Ashworth** – State crime investigator. He has an on-again-off-again friendship with Sheriff Osborne.

Chapter 1

Some evenings I get to aching for the Lantz of my growing up years. I start out kidding myself that it was all fried pickles and lemonade. Then the memories nag and tug on me until I'm right back where all the bleeding and burning started. I'm an old man now leaning in toward eighty. I've made up my mind to tell the whole story just the way it happened. Truth be told, I owe it to the dead ones to set the record straight.

It's best if I start where it started: that morning at the General Store. Seems about right for things to begin at the Store. That pile of timber and tin anchored the crossroads of our pissant town for more than a hundred years. A measly century don't even scratch the surface when you consider that this piece of God's creation has been a meeting-up place for human beings since before Christ was a carpenter. Now if you think that's blasphemy, I'd beg to differ.

You see, there's these archaeologists from The University of Texas in Austin, about sixty miles down the highway from here, who claim prehistoric folk over at the Gault site called this patch of land their home so far back in time they were likely the first humans to set foot on this continent. This came to light when the professors started scraping and sifting through layers of ancient garbage, reclaiming secrets of all those lost generations. When they hit bedrock, they decided they'd found all there was to know and stopped digging.

It puts me in mind of police work. At first, all you get are lies and decaying memory. If you keep after it though, you might just rake up some solid stuff. That's where the scraps of stories and random bits of facts start to make sense. It's there, at the bedrock, where truth rests. Now I've gone to meandering. My Sweet Wife, may she rest in peace, tried to break me from the habit. She never did. If you'll bear with me, I'll get back to the story I set out to tell.

Like I said, it begins at the General Store on the morning in question. If I close my eyes, I can just about picture it same as if it was yesterday.

A bunch of locals are gathered. I'll introduce you around.

Sara Evans is the one filling the coffee cups. Sara lives by her Mama's advice when it comes to men: "Don't get mad. Get even." So, she didn't get mad when she caught Kyle messing around with the two-bit slut from the dry cleaners.

At The Rattlesnake Inn the very night she caught him, three ol' boys had everyone in the joint laughing their fool heads off describing how—ankle-deep in mud—a five-foot-two cowgirl helped them steady the winches and place two-by-fours under the tractor wheels. She'd paid triple so they'd finish the moving job in one day. When Kyle got home that night, he found his clothes, a broken fishing rod, and a hot six-pack stacked on a muddy concrete slab where their double-wide used to sit.

The rest of the people you need to meet are sitting together at the middle table. That's where all the commotion is coming from. The quiet one is Blake Tackett. Blake is one of my Three-B's. We played high school football back in the sixties, the Three B's and me. The other two B's are also at the table.

Now Blake, he has the prettiest place you
closed by miles and miles of board fence, since he ‹
fence worth its salt has to be pig-tight, horse-high, an
His is.

The second B is that tall drink of water standing at ‹
the table, Bobby Seville. Did I mention Bobby's place is 7.
larger than the place owned by his best buddy, Blake? Every‹
Lantz knows this because Bobby is prone to working it into ‹
versations. As usual, Bobby is doing most of the talking. He
ragging on the Number Three B, Buster McCombs. It's a conver·
sation they have on a regular basis because Buster will not do what
needs to be done to clean up the rusted-out heap of junk that lit-
ters his piece-of-shit farm across the road from the Tackett place.

The aforementioned Buster McCombs, B number three, is the
one hunched over nursing a plate of eggs like his gut has a grudge
against chickens. He drips folksy expressions like an old man spitting snuff. He calls our city cemetery the "skeleton orchard," and
if you ask him how he's doing he's likely to growl that he's "fine as
frog's hair." It only takes a few minutes in his company before you
figure out he's just a bowlegged asshole with sour breath and un-
dershorts long past the expiry date.

The final person you need to meet is the eye-catcher sitting
next to her daddy. That would be Miss Lilly Tackett. She's been
Blake's business partner and righthand since she moved home to
Lantz some ten years ago. Some say her nose is a too big for her
face and her blonde hair always looks like it needs to be brushed,
but the boys back in school couldn't keep their hands off her.
What she has going for her are eyes that shift from pale gray to
green to ice blue. Her mama calls it sex appeal and hates her for it.

You've met everyone you need to meet. For now, anyway.

Who am I, you ask? I'm Ray Crawford Osborne, the sumbitch
who had the misfortune to be elected Arrowhead County Sheriff

, as of this morning, it's my job to figure if any of these up-
standing citizens is a murderer.

* * *

Before I go any further, maybe I should step back a couple of
hours and fill you in on how things got to going. I was enjoying
my morning sit down when a call came in over the police car radio.
Sara recently remodeled the outbuildings behind the General
Store, so they offer, bar none, a pair of first class, drive-up privy
stations that are perfect for a man with my particular morning
habits.

The Routine starts with a couple of cups of strong, black coffee. When I say strong, I mean slap-your-mama strong, not that
colored water that some folks brew. Give me a couple of cups of
the good stuff, a newspaper to read, and a little private time and I
get results, if you know what I mean. Bless my Sweet Wife, she
truly does appreciate it when The Routine takes place somewhere
besides home.

The *Austin American-Statesman* was riding on Coach Mac
Brown for allowing the sainted UT Longhorns to lose to the Bay-
lor Bears when I heard the police car radio squeal with the sound
of Katie Sue Brooks' bird voice telling me, in no uncertain terms,
to stop whatever I was doing and pick up because there was serious police business needing my immediate attention. I suppose
she thought if she repeated the call six or eight times, I would understand the urgency.

"Sheriff, we have us a 10-33 out at the Tackett place."

The Routine interrupted, I grabbed the microphone and responded, trying not to sound put out.

"What are you talking about, Katie Sue?"

"Sheriff Ray, you'd better get out to the Tackett place right away."

"What is it?"

"Not for certain but I know it's real bad."

The Tackett place is just a few miles up the road from the Store. That's where I found Johnnie Lake, my part-time deputy, waiting for me on the front porch.

"It's Miss Belle," he said. Miss Belle was what everyone called Veda Tackett, Blake's wife.

"Where's Blake?"

"He and Miss Lilly went to a meeting down in Austin over the weekend. Due back this morning."

The annual meeting of Texas Free Range Cattlemen's Association is a big deal in these parts, and at that time both Bobby and Blake served on the board. Miss Lilly usually accompanied her daddy since Miss Belle made it clear to anyone who would listen just how much she hated hanging out in smelly conference rooms and talking about cows.

"Never mind. They'll go to the General Store when they get back to town. I'll catch up with them there."

Upstairs, Hattie Mae Cooper sat next to the bed where Veda Tackett lay with a chenille bedspread pulled up over her face. Hattie said she'd found the lady of the house in bed when she came to clean and called my office.

"She's gone," Hattie said.

I felt around under the covers for Miss Belle's hand. It was stiff and cold, and although I'm no medical examiner, it was clear she'd been dead for some time. I heard Johnnie shuffling from one foot to the other behind me.

"Who'd you call?" I asked him.

"Georgetown."

Before he could say more, Hattie asked to speak to me alone downstairs in the kitchen. What she showed me changed everything. Seems Miss Belle was fond of a mid-morning mimosa. Hattie always left fresh orange juice in the refrigerator before she finished up in the afternoon. The cut glass juice pitcher she'd left for Miss Belle yesterday was sitting on the counter. Empty. There was a crusty patch in the bottom of pitcher. It had a peculiar smell, more like sour milk than anything that ever grew on a citrus tree.

"There's a glass next to the bed. She musta' drank a lot before she died," Hattie said.

I stared at the pitcher for a long time.

"Shit. Are you kiddin' me?"

You see, county records tell me it's been about seventy-five years since we've had a murder or a suicide in this town. That's if you don't count Catfish Swanson, who died about twenty years ago, as I recall.

Folks back then went out of their way to avoid Gerald "Catfish" Swanson. Some say his nasty disposition and perpetual pout was because he stopped growing at four-foot-four-and-a-half inches. He shocked every living soul in town—man woman and child—when, at the age of forty-two, he came back from a trip up north with a wife. More shocking still was the fact that his bride was six years older than Catfish and nearly two foot taller. She brought a grown daughter with her who was taller still. The story goes that what those two women lacked in looks they made up for in sheer orneriness.

Poor Catfish. No one ever knew, or asked, just exactly how the little man drowned in a rain barrel, head down, feet barely visible above the rim. There wasn't a stepstool or ladder anywhere to be seen. The neighbors were so grateful when the tall ladies sold everything and went back where they came from that nobody asked a lot of questions. Official records counted that one as an "accident."

The Catfish incident was before my time as Sheriff and ain't connected to the case that changed everything in Lantz. I only mention the Catfish case because I want you to understand why we didn't have a lot of practice around these parts with foul play. We are more of a run-off-the-road, shooting accident, die-in-your-sleep kind of place. I, for sure, didn't have experience with suspicious death.

That all changed when somebody went and killed Miss Belle.

CHAPTER 2

I could sense Hattie stifling a snicker as I contemplated the fact that I was face-to-face with an evidence-collecting-potential-crime-scene-securing situation.

"Shit," I said again, not at all embarrassed to be repeating myself. "This is serious. When are the Georgetown folks supposed to get here?"

"Better ask Johnnie. He's the one who called 'em."

"Right."

It's a good thing I watch some CSI on television because I sure didn't remember much from my law enforcement training days.

"Do you have any Ziploc baggies?"

Hattie was way ahead of me. She'd pulled an assortment from the pantry while I was studying the orange juice pitcher.

"Right. Now don't touch anything."

"Yes, Sir!" she replied, giving me a mock salute and a grin that made me relax a bit. You gotta love Hattie.

We found a pair of disposable rubber gloves for each of us, and I fetched a camera from the patrol car. Upstairs I took photos of the layout of the nightstand and collected the champagne flute into a baggie the way I'd seen it done on TV. I figured the team from Georgetown would do the rest. Right now, I needed to get a look at the body.

With Hattie's help I pulled down the bedspread and gave Miss Belle a quick once-over, trying to be as respectful as I could under the circumstances. She wore a frilly nylon nightgown and bed jacket, all ribbons and bows, tied up close around her chubby neck. Her feet were covered with pink, crocheted booties. The bottoms were clean, so I figured she hadn't left the bed since she laid down. I started to pull the bedspread back up when Hattie offered a suggestion.

"You might want to check the safe."

I must have looked confused because she shook her head.

"Didn't your mama teach you anything? All the well-endowed ladies around here stow things in their bra where it's handy," she said.

Before I could stop her, Hattie reached under the bed jacket between Miss Belle's bosoms and felt around. Rumpled tissues and ChapStick lip balm were all she found at first pass.

"Miss Belle decided she ought to wear a sleep bra back when her girls started to settle," Hattie said. "She was determined to fight gravity as she began to lose her girlish figure."

After another excavation she held up a folded piece of blue stationery.

I opened a Ziploc for her to deposit the ChapStick and tissues. I unfolded the stationery for a peek. It was a handwritten note.

Just a few words. Could mean anything. Could mean nothing. Could mean everything.

"I know what you did. Call me. B."

Shit. Double shit.

Naturally, Johnnie was looking over my shoulder again and let out a long, slow whistle before I'd re-folded the paper and slipped it into its own baggie.

"Now, Johnnie, you know this is official police business. You cannot repeat anything we've found here. It could hurt our investigation." I tried to sound official, but to my ears the word "investigation" sounded as if I was putting on airs.

Thank God Almighty, the Georgetown team arrived before I hit full-bore panic mode. I explained my initial assessment and they called for backup from the Department of Public Safety investigators in Austin. Before long we had the whole crime-scene-tape brigade on the way. I told them I would go to the Store to notify the next of kin.

This time of the morning, working folks around here gather at the Store to trade lies and cuss politicians. Some mornings I join them. It's a good way to catch up on what's going on around the county.

On this particular morning, I'd be the one telling the story and I'd be the one asking the questions. That's why I stood outside to collect my thoughts before opening the door. Inside were some friends of mine. They all had a reason to love Miss Belle. They all had a reason to hate her. Worse still, they all had a reason to want her dead.

CHAPTER 3

You might say the shit hit the proverbial fan after I delivered the news. Buster McCombs bailed out the back door like the sorry so-and-so he is. When I delivered the news of her mother's death, Miss Lilly Tackett let out such a scream it set my ears to ringing. Then she grabbed her keys, jumped up, ran to her truck. Bobby Seville was close behind her, but Miss Lilly has a reputation of driving faster than Dale Earnhardt on steroids so I figured Bobby wouldn't catch her.

In typical Blake fashion, Miss Belle's husband didn't move, didn't cry, didn't say a word. He sat there without moving a muscle. Trying to process the news, I suppose.

Sara, the chief cook and bottle washer for the Store, topped off Blake's coffee and sat down next to him. The front door was still rattling a bit from Miss Lilly's exit.

I had to make a quick lawman decision. Go after Lilly and Bobby? Chase Buster? Or stay with Sara and Blake? Seemed to me I might get some good leads from these two if I eased in across from them, so that's what I did.

"Blake," I started. "I'm sorry for your loss."

He didn't reply so I gave him a minute before adding, "We're going to need to sort a few things out."

Sara gave me a look that sent ice traveling up my legs and settling in my nether regions. It was an unspoken threat certain women know how to deliver without opening their mouth. My Aunt Durrell had that talent. My sister does, too. I do pity her husband.

"This is police business, Sara."

"It's okay," Blake said, reaching for his coffee cup. His stopped short of actually taking a drink. He sat holding the cup suspended near his chin for a strange amount of time until he took a deep breath and returned the cup to the table. He ran his hand over his close-clipped gray hair and reached for his hat.

"Suppose we should go now," he finally said. The words came out slow as if he'd chewed on each one. The result was more like a question than a statement.

When Blake and I pulled up at the Tackett place, we had trouble finding a close-in spot to park. The motor was still running on Miss Lilly's truck and the door was hanging open. Her speed in getting there from the General Store had not been rewarded because the investigators were prohibiting anyone from entering the house. She was making quite a scene, walking from one person to the other, her arms jabbing the air, demanding in an impassioned voice that they let her inside the house to see her mother. Bobby was trailing behind making the same request in a more polite way. Neither of them was having any success making a case with the officials who'd taken command of the Tackett place since I left.

Hattie was on the front porch talking to a uniformed officer. I counted four police units on the lawn and driveway. All from out of town. My lazy-ass, part-time deputy, Johnnie Lake, was nowhere to be seen. Typical.

Lucky for me, I spotted Phillip Ashworth right away. He was easy to pick out from the crowd because he's a bit over six feet tall and bears an uncanny resemblance to the film actor Matthew McConaughey. Phil and I go back a ways. His cousin is married to my wife's brother, so you might say we are semi-cousins. We've shared more than one weekend on a deer blind so I can look past his flaws, one of which is graduation from Texas Tech. No one is perfect and I try to be broadminded enough to accept that in Texas there will always be some people foolish enough to drive all the way to Lubbock to get a college degree. A few, you might try to argue, are even necessary. Personally, I've always thought there was some truth in that lyric about happiness being Lubbock, Texas, in your rearview mirror.

Phil works at the Department of Public Safety headquarters in Austin. He started out in forensics but has worked his way up to detective status. Don't ask me to explain it. You know how bureaucrats are. Some days it seems they spend almost as much time rearranging organizational charts and making up fancy new titles as they do actually solving crime. Don't make a hell of a lotta sense to folks like me who earn their paycheck. Like I said, Phil is one of the good ones. That's why I was glad to see him.

I tipped my hat to Phil, and he gave me the Tech Red Raider guns up hand signal greeting. For those of you who are uninitiated in such rituals let's just say it resembles a backwards "L" and may as well be one. He does it to annoy me. I returned the favor with a University of Texas Hook 'em Horns, the university's two-finger Longhorn salute. If there happened to be someone from out-of-state watching, they'd swear we were trading obscene gestures.

Phil waved me over to a group of fellow officers, introducing me all around.

"This is Arrowhead's own Sheriff Ray Crawford Osborne," he told them. "I've been trying to get him to apply to the Rangers, but you can't pry this man out of Arrowhead County."

"I was born here and likely will die here," I said with what I hoped was a friendly tone. Then I proceeded to fill them in on Hattie's call to the office, what I'd found in the kitchen, and what turned up in Miss Belle's "safe."

"Until your crime lab tells me what's in the pitcher, I can't be sure this was poison, but I don't think Miss Belle was drinking alone last night," I told them.

"Why do you say that?" Phil asked.

Before I could answer, Lilly came dashing up and grabbed my arm.

"Ray, this is crazy. They won't let me see my Mama. Tell them."

I took her hand and answered as gently as I could, "They need to do what they need to do, Miss Lilly. You have to give them some time."

Blake came up behind his daughter and put a protective arm around her shoulder. "Ray, this is my house. They can't keep us out, can they?"

"Standard police procedure," I explained and then turned to Phil and introduced Blake and Lilly. "These are the next of kin. I think we can at least find a comfortable place for them to wait."

Hattie joined us and asked Phil if she could make his crew some coffee. He told her the kitchen was temporarily off limits until they finished sweeping it for evidence.

"Something you might have mentioned before I wet mopped the floor," she said, shaking her head as she walked away.

Before Miss Lilly could treat us to another tirade, Phil escorted her inside to the dining room and a uniformed officer took Blake to the den. Since Blake looked like he was drifting in and out of a catatonic cloud, I decided to join Phil and Lilly. To be honest, I've always been a little intimidated by Lilly. It would be interesting to see how a pro like Phil handled a firebrand like her. After half an hour, Phil gave up. He never got a helpful word in edgewise. Said he would try again when Lilly was calmer. Hell, I could've done that.

Phil and I walked up the driveway a piece to give us a private place to talk out of earshot of the others.

"Any preliminary thoughts on who might have had it in for Miss Belle?" he asked.

"I have my suspicions, but I need to talk to some people, establish alibis and the like," I told him.

We made a quick decision that I'd handle initial interviews with what he called the "locals." He'd wrap things up at the crime scene and then go back to Austin to start the paperwork, get the evidence processed, and expedite the autopsy. We agreed to talk before the end of the day. Seemed right to me.

CHAPTER 4

I came to realize just how hard my job would be as I watched Blake standing next to the empty bed that only a short time before had held the body of his wife.

Phil's team finally let Lilly and Blake go upstairs to say their farewells before they prepared Miss Belle's body for transport. For their peace of mind, I'm grateful Miss Belle still looked okay. Her color was off but she didn't show any outward signs of distress. The two of them had walked up to the bed hand in hand. Miss Lilly kissed her mama's forehead, stroked her cheek, and then exited as though she couldn't take much more. Blake stood there looking down at Belle, his face white and cold. He touched the fingertips of his right hand to his lips and then softly pressed them to each of her eyelids.

The mortuary team asked Blake to step out into the hall to give them a chance to finish wrapping her body. I had a strong sense he felt that he owed it to his wife to bear witness so he stayed close. Out of respect, I stood with him. We watched while they worked.

Miss Belle would have hated strangers seeing her in her night-dress, would have hated stranger's hands on her body as they wrapped her in transport sheets. I fear the sheets were made of muslin. She would have hated that, too. Everyone knew she only bought Egyptian cotton with the highest thread count. They knew because Belle was the type of woman who talked about labels and costs. As the saying goes, she knew the price of everything and the value of nothing.

The mortuary folks stretched sheets around her like a mummy. Left to right, top to bottom, over and under, until she was bound up taut enough to bounce a quarter off her rear. She would have hated that. Finally, they were ready to lift her onto the gurney.

"On the count of three. One. Two. Three."

Up and over; strange hands clicked the railing into place with a sharp screech of metal on metal. She'd have hated that sound. Miss Belle kept cans of WD-40 stashed around the place in case any doors or cabinets had the sass to squeak in her presence. Such a thing was no more tolerated by Miss Belle than a man who would break wind at the dinner table.

It took all three of the men to negotiate the serpentine stairs, bumping the gurney and leaving marks on the walls as they bounced down each tread. Miss Belle would have hated that, too.

Once they exited, Blake went back in the bedroom and stood looking at the empty king-sized bed.

"Guess your hating days are over," Blake said softly to the spot on the mattress where his wife had laid just minutes before. He smoothed the bedspread across the vacant place, fluffed up the pillows, and patted them into shape.

The floor-to-ceiling windows in the bedroom offered a yawning view of the northern pasture. The Tackett driveway circled around to a six-bay service garage where Blake parked his tractors, combines, harvesters, and other such equipment. If you were from around here, you'd know most folks leave such stuff parked in the field. Blake is not most folk.

He was studying on his garage when I eased up behind him. We are about the same height and age, but standing there with his back to me and his shoulders slumped, he seemed smaller and older. He didn't turn around.

"Paint's peeling under the eaves," he said.

"Where?"

"Should have done it myself. Half-ass job."

"We still need to talk about what happened."

"I know."

"Let's go downstairs."

Blake followed me, pausing to give the bedroom one last look before switching off the light.

I've known that man since we played high school ball. He was a tight end and I started as linebacker. Neither one of us was much good, if truth be told. Like most high schoolers, we liked the uniforms and hellraising so much that the score didn't much matter at the end of the day.

There was this one night I remember in particular. It was after an unfortunate trouncing by the Hutto Hippos, when the Three B's and I got shit-faced on Shiner with tequila chasers. We parked on FM 970, where Buster and Bobby promptly threw up. Then, for reasons with no purchase in logic, the two of them began to argue over which one of their mamas made the best banana pudding.

It was one of those nights where the stars and moon give off enough light to see by. Blake and I walked up the road a bit to get away from the smell. We didn't have to go too far 'til we found a comfortable tree to squat under.

What I contributed in the way of conversation probably was on the order of how we'd been cheated by those good-for-nothing refs and which of the cheerleaders I would like to do what with.

You know, the kind of meaningless things boys of that particular age tend to consider witty repartee.

Blake, as I recall, turned all philosophical. I don't remember everything he said. I do, however, remember him talking about dying. Seems his problem wasn't whether there's a hereafter. His problem was the whole "When" aspect of dying. Seems the unknowable aspect about the timing was a constant annoyance that bugged him.

"Uncertainty is the real bitch," he said. How to plan properly was his concern. How much money will you need? Do you take a trip, or can you put it off until next year? Plant sorghum or corn? If you only knew how much time you had it would be easier to make decisions.

"In a way," he said, "I envy those folks on death row in Huntsville. At least at some point they know the When and the How and the Where. How comforting it must be to be able to make clear, unambiguous plans."

Like I said, pretty deep stuff for a high school senior. Kinda makes you wonder.

I thought about that night as I escorted him down the stairs. By the time we reached the living room, Blake's legs seemed to turn to rubber. I grabbed hold of his arm and helped him to the couch, where he slumped over with his elbows resting on his knees and studied the pattern in the rug. I could see he was slipping away when Hattie pulled me to one side.

"If you give him a bit of space, you'll get a heck of a lot more out of him than if you keep ragging on him right now," she said.

"Think so?"

"I know so. Give the man a little time to wrap his head around all this," she said with a wave encompassing all the police tape and disarray of where crews from Austin had invaded the house. "Come back later. You're his friend. He'll talk with you."

I slipped over and put a friendly hand on Blake's shoulder telling him I'd check in later. I'm pretty sure he didn't hear me.

"Where's Miss Lilly now?" I asked Hattie.

"Leave that child to me," Hattie said. "You go do your lawman thing."

CHAPTER 5

I drove straight to the General Store only to find a sign on the locked door that told me it wouldn't reopen until 1 p.m. Sara hadn't bothered to explain the unexpected midday closing. That's the Store for you.

R.W. Seville, Bobby's only child and his namesake, was leaning back in a rocking chair on the front porch, nursing a Dr Pepper, his boots propped up on the porch railing. R.W. has his daddy's build, all leg and no butt. It's too soon to know if he'll hang on to his full head of curly black hair or lose it the way Bobby did. R.W. is possibly the only human being who can out-talk Bobby. The two of them have been known to have a thirty-minute conversation in six minutes flat. When he saw me, R.W. dropped his feet off the railing and stood up, pointing the bottom of his soda bottle at the sign on the door.

"Store's closed, Sheriff Ray."

"I can see that, R.W."

"You think it's because of Miss Belle? Everyone in town is talking about what happened over at the Tackett place." He got up and tossed his empty bottle in the trash barrel and gave the door handle a good shake to confirm it was locked.

"Why aren't you with the other laws?" he asked. "Seems you would be right in the thick of it."

"Just came from there."

Since my agreement with Phil was to take the lead on questioning locals, R.W. was as good a start as any.

"You up for an early lunch?" I proposed.

I figured R.W. would relax if he was somewhere familiar, and Joe's Place was the perfect ticket. I offered to drive both of us to Jarrell, hometown to the original Joe's.

Joe's Place is my go-to greasy burger joint. No one in their right mind can refuse one of his double-double cheeseburgers fresh off the grill. He had a chain of four joints in various towns until he split with his wife, Flo. He was left with two establishments in the divorce settlement. She changed the signage on her two to "Flo's Place." Menu didn't change, only the name. It was clever the way the sign painter fancied up the "Joe" into a "Flo." Michelangelo had nothing on him.

What you must do is eat your Joe's burgers right as they come off the grill. If you try takeout, the grease will soak through the paper bag before you get home. You can do it, but it ain't pretty. One night, I'd had one too many cold ones as I watched Joe ball up the ground meat and slap it on the grill. Then he took his spatula and gave the ball of meat a good whack. The result was a patty with a superfluousness of uneven shoreline. Watching it sizzle and pop, I developed my theory, which, given my advanced state of inebriation I felt compelled to share with Joe.

"Joe, my man," I told him. "I have a theory."

"And what would that be?"

"Have you ever noticed all the extra edging on your burger patties?"

"I can't say that I have," he said, flipping the meat and giving the patty another pounding, creating new estuaries and gullies in addition to squirting more grease onto his well-oiled apron.

"It is my understanding your franchise joints such as your Dairy Queen and your Whataburger use pre-fab, frozen patties. This produces nice, even patty edges. Now as I see it, this limits the overall circumference to your grease absorption possibilities while on the grill and, thus, compromises the finished burger flavor. Your method, on the other hand, provides an ultimate grease-soaking ratio. That, my friend, is why a Joe's burger tastes like this side of heaven."

"Whatever you say, Ray. Whatever you say. You've always been the one with the eye for details and a way of putting two and two together," Joe nodded, sliding a heaping plate of hot cheeseburger and waffle fries across the counter to me.

I used the ten-mile drive from the Store to Joe's to open the conversation with R.W. about Miss Belle's last day.

"Damn shame about Miss Belle," I told him. "I know you'll miss her."

"I can't get my head around the fact that she's gone," he said reaching for the car radio dial. "Okay if I try to get us a country & western station on this?"

"Better leave it be. I need to listen in on the police scanner."

"Sure. Sorry."

"I know how close you were. You and Miss Belle."

"I guess so. Lilly and I practically grew up together after my mama passed," R.W. said, his eyes fixed on the view out the window. After a pause, he surprised me with a question that seemed to come out of nowhere. "Did you ever notice her hands?"

"Who?"

"Miss Belle."

"Can't say that I did."

"Her hands are big. That's why she wore those stout rings, the kind you couldn't find in a jewelry store. Two were made of pearls and diamonds. One was made of the biggest coral pieces I've ever seen. She told me that she had it specially made from Blake's old cuff links. It was her favorite. She called them her trophies."

I made a mental note to ask Lilly about the rings.

After we arrived at Joe's and placed our order, I decided to let R.W. keep on doing most of the talking while we sipped our drinks.

"I'm going over to sit with Lilly tonight. Austin folks treated her pretty rough," he said, pulling the paper from his straw. He stroked the length of it with a single practiced motion, using his Texas A&M University class ring to smooth it out before rolling the paper up to resemble an origami snail.

"They're good guys," I replied, fudging a bit. In all honesty, the only DPS investigator who I could testify as to having a lick of sense was Phil Ashworth.

I watched R.W. fiddle with the condiments on the table. He lined up the ketchup and Tabasco packets and then moved the salt and peppershakers into a neat row, so their labels faced the same direction. He played around with the napkins, folding, and smoothing out all the wrinkles.

All that fidgeting was getting on my last nerve when Joe saved the day by delivering our food. Then R.W. started in again, folding the waxed paper wrapper on his double cheeseburger creasing it evenly all around. The one thing he didn't do was eat.

"Not hungry?" I asked him.

"Lilly's almost hysterical."

"What do you mean?"

"They're gonna do a full autopsy," he said. "Lilly pitched a fit when she heard about it. She's seen stuff on those TV cop shows about how they cut people up and take out their insides."

"They don't have a lot of choice in a case like this. The law requires a postmortem whenever there is an unnatural, suspicious, or unattended death. They'll respect Miss Belle's dignity," I said.

"Lilly screamed at her daddy something awful. She told him that if he loved her or cared two cents about Miss Belle, he'd put a stop to it."

"Where did you hear that?"

The words were no sooner out of my mouth than I could tell from R.W.'s reaction that my tone reminded him that despite the familiar location and soda pop, this was an official police interview. His shoulders stiffened and he clammed up.

"Son, I asked you a question. When did Miss Lilly talk to her father about Belle's autopsy? It's a simple question."

He decided to take an interest in his waffle fries, swirling them one at a time in a ketchup pool. "Not sure."

"Come on. Did you hear the conversation? Were you there? Did she call you? Help me here."

"I guess it don't matter if I tell you. I called her to see how she was doing. We hung up just before you arrived at the Store. No big deal."

"Okay. That's better." I made a show of jotting something on my notepad to give him a chance to eat a few fries before asking the next question. "When was the last time you saw her?"

"Lilly?"

"Miss Belle."

"Last night, I guess."

"You say you saw Miss Belle last night?"

"We ate supper and watched a movie together."

"What time was it?"

"I'd say six o'clock or so."

"Tell me about it."

He said that he and Belle had a regular movie date on Sunday nights. He brought her some sliced brisket from Stubb's Bar-B-Q and honky-tonk in Austin, and they watched *Midnight Cowboy*.

"We've been doing movie night since I was about twelve years old," he said. "Sometimes Lilly would join us. Mostly it was Miss Belle and me."

"What kind of movies did you watch?"

"Mostly the ones from the sixties and seventies. I've seen *Space Odyssey, Strangelove, Bonnie & Clyde, Breakfast at Tiffany's* all at least a dozen times. Sometimes we would act out parts. Got to where we'd talk over the actors and pretend we were in a scene. Like she'd be Bonnie and I'd be Clyde. Or I'd give the Atticus Finch courtroom speech in *Mockingbird*. It was fun. She was fun."

His voice faded off as if he realized he was speaking in past tense. "I'm gonna miss movie nights."

"Not everyone saw that side of Miss Belle."

He didn't respond at first, nibbling at his burger before speaking. "I know what you're getting at. I'll be the first to admit that she could be nettlesome. Some people thought there was a meanness about her. That's because she always said what she meant and never apologized. Ever."

"Did she have something to apologize for?"

"Depends on who you talk to," he said, a small grin on his face. "Did you hear what happened at the last church bake sale?"

My Sweet Wife had given me the full skinny on the bake sale, but I decided to play dumb.

"I understand the Ladies' Auxiliary made a nice haul. Set a new record."

"Well, what I had in mind was the pineapple cake Mrs. Frierson baked. Now you know that family lives on a shoestring because he has trouble keeping a regular job and they have those five kids and all. Mrs. Frierson usually makes a jam cake to sell. You see, she always brags about how she saves up all the bits of leftover jam to flavor her pound cake. Miss Belle made an offhand remark about how it would be nice if Mrs. Frierson tried something besides her usual 'scraps cake,' as she called it. Mrs. Frierson was so mortified she got talked into making that pineapple cake since almost no one can really afford it. What with four cups of pecans and heaps of cream cheese icing, ingredients alone must cost a small fortune."

"Mrs. Frierson could have said 'no.'"

"That's just it. You can't say 'no' to Miss Belle. No one can. Anyway, while I was helping set up tables for the sale, I overheard Miss Belle gossiping about how the Frierson kitchen was rumored to have a cockroach problem."

Before I could respond, Joe walked over to our table.

"Problem with the food, boys?"

I told him nothing whatsoever could ever be wrong with his burgers. "We got caught up in conversation."

"Damn shame about Miss Belle," he said as he left. "Don't let your sandwiches get cold or they won't be fit to feed to the hogs."

"You got that right," I yelled after Joe and then turned back to R.W.

"You heard the man," I told him. "Eat."

R.W. began to work on his food as he continued the story.

"I'm not sure anyone believed Miss Belle about the roaches, but they got the message. The upshot was no one was bidding on Mrs. Frierson's cake during the silent auction. Poor Mrs. Frierson was nearly in tears."

"Why are you telling me this, R.W.? Do you think it has something to do with Miss Belle's death?"

"Oh, God, no. She had a way of messing with people, that's all," he said, taking a big bite of burger, then dipping some waffle fries into catsup. After a few more bites, he shrugged. "I suppose it all worked out for Mrs. Frierson in the end."

"How so?"

"About the time the bidding was about to close, someone wrote down an anonymous bid for $250. That pineapple cake set an all-time record. Mrs. Frierson was the talk of the sale."

"Did Miss Belle mention the cake when you were together last night?"

"She did. She said when she got home from the bake sale that pineapple cake was sitting in her kitchen with a note. 'I know how much you love pineapple. B.' She said she tossed the whole cake in the trash."

"You say you don't think the cake sale had anything to do with what happened to Miss Belle, but you thought I needed to hear the story anyway?"

"It was preying on my mind, that's all," he said, polishing off his burger and folding up the wax paper it came wrapped in. "Excellent."

"Do you know of anyone who would want to do her harm?"

"I couldn't really say."

"Now that is a sure enough ambiguous response to the question. Are you trying to tell me you don't know or you're not willing to talk about it?"

My words must have come out with more annoyance than I intended because R.W.'s face turned a darker shade of red.

"Sorry, son," I said. "Didn't mean to jump on you. I know this is tough."

R.W. tried to recover his composure and I repeated my question.

"Do you know anyone who would want to do her harm?"

"I can't tell you anything you don't already know. Sure, she ruffled people's feathers and she wasn't the kind to apologize if she hurt your feelings. It's hard to imagine someone would be so mean as to actually hurt her."

"You said something like that before. Do you think Miss Belle owed someone an apology?"

"Don't we all? If you're not careful, I suppose poison has a way of catching up with you."

I'd tried to avoid taking notes while R.W. talked because I didn't want to break his concentration, but I did jot down a reminder about his poison comment. I've learned it's best to let people keep talking to see where it will lead. Journalists and police share a secret about human nature. Sometimes the best way to get people to spill the beans is to shut up and let them talk. Brow beating makes people defensive. Silence can turn on the flood. While he finished his soda, I let R.W. continue to control the conversation.

"There was a comfort, I suppose, in her bluntness, in knowing where you stood with her. It was also kinda scary. She was like a loaded gun with a hair trigger, and you were always a little afraid one day it would be pointed at you when it went off."

"Was it?"

"What?"

"Ever pointed at you?"

His face turned red again and his breathing skipped a beat or two. When he did answer, he talked slower, as if he needed each thought to dry out before he let it out of his mouth. "No, never me. She liked to tell me stories about other people, but we, Miss Belle and me, were always friends."

I could see that I needed to wrap up my questions. "How was Miss Belle when you left last night?"

"About as usual. I helped her clean up after the movie. She said she was going to go to bed."

"What time did you leave?'

"Around 9:30."

"Did you go straight home?"

"Yeah. I was tired. Long day."

"Was Bobby home?"

"Sure. Daddy's always in bed before ten. We have to get up early."

"Are you sure?'

"Of course, I'm sure. His truck was in the driveway."

That wasn't the only lie R.W. told, but it was a big one.

CHAPTER 6

The General Store was humming when I dropped R.W. off. A band of middle-aged bikers filled two communal tables, and Sara was running herself ragged serving up sandwiches and sweet tea. Buster was hunched down at his usual spot in the rear of the Store.

The clean-shaven bikers gave me a sheepish look when they spotted my badge and side arm. I offered a friendly nod to put them at ease. Recreational motorcyclists are a common sight around here. They're mostly dentists, lawyers, realtors, and such who like to dust the cobwebs off their $60,000 rides, pull on the leathers, and take their bad boys out for a cruise when the sky is blue and the wind is down. Harmless. Only trouble they were likely to get into that day would be if they tried to strike up a conversation with Buster. He looked as if he'd already been throwing back a few too many and was itching for a fight.

My first stop was at the front counter, a genuine vintage diner relic. Sara managed to keep the floor-to-ceiling shelving along the southern wall of the Store stocked with the kind of everyday necessities and knickknacks that assured a regular income. Canned goods, pantry basics, and Cheerios seemed right at home next to light bulbs, laundry soap, screws, and batteries. It was the vintage dining counter that gave the Store its character. Most of the important parts were salvaged from a soda fountain when a drug store in downtown Killeen was torn down after World War II. The deep stainless-steel sinks, sandwich board, grill, and moss green Formica countertop had all been seasoned with decades of use and loving care.

"Don't have time for you right now, Ray. I've got bigger fish to fry. Come by the house after I close," Sara called out over her shoulder without turning around from her work at the sandwich line. "You have to let me earn a living while I can."

"Not a problem," I replied, making my way to the back of the Store. I eased onto the bench across from Buster. He kept his face buried in his lunch.

"Let's go out back where we can talk," I said to the top of his ball cap.

"Is that an order?"

"If you need it to be."

Buster looked up and glared at the two bikers nearest to us. "What are you ass wipes looking at?"

They gave him a nervous look, got up and moved to another table.

"Let's do this easy, Buster. No sense making trouble."

He grabbed his beer and sandwich and headed out the rear door. I tipped my hat to the bikers. "You boys have a nice day."

I wasn't one hundred percent sure Buster wouldn't keep on moving after he cut out the back door, so I was kinda surprised to find him waiting for me at a table under a live oak tree. I settled in across from him and gave him a few minutes to work on his lunch.

Watching Buster eat is not the way you'd volunteer to spend too much time. His table manners were never polished and had grown worse as he aged. No one had bothered to teach him the basics, like closing your mouth when you chew, or what to eat with a fork instead of your hands, or how to pull off small bits of bread rather than stuff the whole slice in your mouth. When he eats a fat sandwich, the innards will ooze out the backside. He hunkers over a bowl of chili with his elbows on the table so he can use his spoon like a backhoe digger, shoveling in huge gulps. And don't get me started on the life forms that undoubtedly germinate in his beard because of the fertilizer he supplies from food that drips there and never gets wiped away.

I know these are things that I have no business criticizing since, if you ask my Sweet Wife, I'm not exactly blessed with impeccable manners. But damn, man, would it kill you to brush your teeth occasionally? And the way he uses food to point at you is an appetite-killer, especially since his fingernails are long and an unnatural color of shale.

Then there's the nose hair. Now in the ordinary course of the day I spend no time at all thinking about nose hair. That is until I'm in the company of Buster. Then I can become mesmerized by the tight tufts of hair crowding his nostrils and poking out in every direction. The hair that curls around and over his ears is greasy and thin, but his nose hair is gray and stiff. Makes you wonder how air can still pass through that undergrowth.

"How are things at the Tackett place?" he asked without looking up.

"About like you might expect."

"As Daddy used to say, 'something's got to get ya.'"

"Or someone?"

He kept working on his corn chips without making eye contact.

"I need to ask a few questions," I told him.

"Shoot."

"Tell me about yesterday. Where were you?"

He picked up his beer and took a long, slow drink. "Well, now, let me see. I got up about eight and fed the pups. Then I took a satisfying dump. Then I decided to drive over to Florence. On the way, I stopped off here for some coffee and Sara's homemade sweet rolls. Since she didn't have any other customers, we talked for a bit."

"What did you talk about?"

"What difference does it make?"

"You're right, it may not matter, but tell me anyway."

"Well, if you want to know the truth, I was filling her in on a chat I had with a pipeline company that wants an easement across my back forty. Could mean a nice piece of change for me."

"You don't say?"

Did I mention Buster has a nervous habit of making a gesture with his fingers and thumb? He does it with his right hand. It's like he's counting. He taps each finger with his thumb, starting with his pinky, touching each digit, and then starting again. When he'd finished his sandwich, he started that tapping business. It took all my will power not to grab his hand and order him to stop. Gets on my last nerve.

"What then?" I asked.

"Over to Florence to meet the boys at the VFW. We had some business to discuss about the Veteran's Memorial. Then some of us drove over to The Rattlesnake for lunch. Good Ol' Tony can vouch for me."

His finger tapping picked up tempo.

"What then?"

"You sure are a nosy sumbitch."

"Just doing my job, Buster. How did you spend the rest of the day?"

"Not much of the day left. We kinda kept drinking until it was time to go home. Tony can vouch for me."

"So you said. What time did you get home?"

"Don't know for sure."

"Did anyone go with you to Sara's house or were you by yourself?"

His thumb tapping stopped and the veins on the bridge of his nose turned a deeper shade of purple.

"What are you talking about?"

"Look at your hand."

The back of his hand was covered in deep scratches. They were fresh. We both knew where they'd come from.

"You don't miss much, do you, Sheriff?"

"That's why they pay me the big bucks."

CHAPTER 7

Hattie was on the porch with a watering can when I turned off the highway to the Tackett place. She waved at me and watched as I negotiated the circular gravel driveway and parked.

"Bougainvillea," she said, indicating the startling magenta, orange and purple flowers in heavy baskets suspended from hooks attached to the fascia of the wrap-around porch. "Miss Belle loved her some bougainvillea."

Hattie sat down on the top step and I joined her. "Figured you'd be back."

"How's Blake doing?"

"Over there," she said pointing to the north field where I could make him out in the distance on his riding mower. "Nothing needed cutting, he just needed to be doing something."

"Where's Miss Lilly?"

"Upstairs in her Mama's room. She's put on one of her mama's frilly nightgowns and covered herself in Miss Belle's signature fragrance. It's Youth Dew body cream by Estée Lauder."

From the glint in her eye, I could see that Hattie, out of respect, was fighting to hold back a smirk. I believe I knew that she was thinking it had been a couple of decades since Miss Belle qualified as "youthful" anywhere except in her own vanity.

"Last time I looked in," Hattie said, "Lilly was curled up in a chair with an album of old family photos from her childhood. I fixed her a pimento cheese sandwich, but I don't expect she will touch it."

"How about you?"

"I'm maintaining."

Before she said more, she stood up and pointed to a three-car caravan making its way off the road and through the Tackett gate.

"Well, here they come," she sighed.

"Who?"

"The church ladies. I've been expecting them. Don't you just know the widows in three counties started baking pies and making appointments at the beauty parlor the minute they got wind of what happened to Miss Belle. A fresh widower is a catch and a half. They'll be on him like stink on a skunk." She picked up the watering can and started for the front door.

"Those ladies are probably packing enough fried chicken, deviled eggs, and noodle casseroles to feed Coxey's Army," she said. "I'd better go clean out the fridge, and you'd better warn Blake."

I didn't need to be told twice. Blake was making a swing toward the house. I waved at him and motioned toward an ancient live oak near the fenceline. When he saw the church ladies pulling up, he made a quick U-turn and drove toward the tree.

In the time it took me to reach him, he'd dismounted and found a soft spot to sit, his back against the trunk. He'd pulled a package of cigarettes from his pocket and was lighting up. I didn't want to get my uniform dirty, so I leaned against the mower. He offered me a smoke, but I declined. Neither of us said anything for a while. I was the first to break the silence.

"Didn't realize you were smoking again."

"Belle didn't like it," he said, taking a long draw and then holding the cigarette out from him to study the burning tip. "Doesn't matter now."

"Sorry for your loss."

"You already said," Blake said, taking off his hat and mopping sweat from his forehead with his pocket handkerchief.

"Wasn't sure you heard me."

"I hear most things. Like that conversation you were having with your Austin buddy."

"Phillip Ashworth?"

"I heard them boys from Austin talking about something in Belle's orange juice. Said they thought she'd killed herself. Well, I can tell you right now, that's not Belle's way."

"They have to look at all the possibilities."

"What do you mean by 'they?' You're right in the middle of it, Sheriff Osborne."

I didn't like the salty tone in his voice. Blake and I had been friends since we were in Cub Scouts. In all the years I'd worn the badge he'd never once called me "Sheriff."

"By 'possibilities,' you mean you think there is something wrong with the way Belle died. You think someone killed her, don't you, Sheriff?"

There it was again, that tone, as if the word itself was an insult.

"You are not here as my friend," he said, taking a long draw from his cigarette. "You are here to question Lilly and me like we are low-life suspects. If someone hurt Belle, Sheriff, it wasn't me and it sure as hell wasn't Lilly."

"No one is accusing you or Miss Lilly of anything. I have a job to do. I have to ask a few questions."

"Like what?"

"Like where everyone was last night. That way I can put together the pieces and figure out what happened to your wife. At this stage it's only questions. That's all. Questions."

Blake stood and flicked his cigarette to the ground, putting it out with the heel of his boot. He remounted his mower and started driving away. He was a few yards into the field when he turned around. He got off the mower and picked up the spent butt and put it in his pocket.

"Meet you out back at the shed. We can talk there."

It wasn't a long walk, but by the time I arrived Blake had hosed off the tires on his mower and parked it in the shed. He was busy sorting and wrapping scrap wire and loose cord piled in a bin on his workbench.

"Pull up a seat," he said, indicating a stool next to him. "Helps if I stay busy."

I watched him work for a bit before pulling out my notebook.

"Fill me in on yesterday."

"Belle and I ate an early breakfast before I left for Austin. She knew I planned to spend the night after the Cattlemen's meeting."

"How did she seem?"

"What do you mean?"

"Was she upset about anything? Did she mention any particular plans for the day?"

"I've thought about it long and hard since you told me she was gone. I don't recall much at all. If I had known it was the last time I would see her I swear I would have paid closer attention. I was thinking about other things and she was talking and talking, the way she always did. I guess I tuned most of it out."

"I'm especially curious if she mentioned plans for the day. Any company she might be expecting. Things like that."

"If she did, I don't remember. She was always going on about plans with her lady friends. I didn't always pay close attention to her."

He cleaned out the now empty bin using spray cleaner and reached for a can of nuts and bolts. Before emptying them on the workbench, he turned to me.

"I know it sounds bad, Ray. Especially now. You know how it is, don't you?"

I didn't know how to answer. I just watched as he began sorting the contents of the can.

"How did things go in Austin?" I finally asked, flipping to another page in my notebook.

"Typical Association meeting. Board members fighting over money in the morning. Guest speakers after lunch. There was this one fella from the federal government telling us all about a big ass fence they're building down on parts of the border like we were supposed to think it would stop illegal traffic. What they don't know about fences. I swear," Blake said with a withering groan. "Makes your blood boil. Mark my words, before it's all said and done it will be another government boondoggle."

"Anything else?"

"Not much. Mostly backslapping and bragging over drinks after the meetings broke up. The food was pretty good."

"When did you get back to Lantz?"

He raked each stack of bolts he'd sorted into a separate baggie before he answered.

"I went to the Store for coffee this morning because I promised to meet Lilly there. Bobby was there, too. But then you know all that."

"You didn't stop by your house first?"

"I wish to God Almighty I had."

Blake's shoulders sagged and his skin took on an ashen tinge. It wasn't lost on me that he really hadn't answered my question. It looked as if he was going to drift away again when he asked me a question.

"When did it all go to hell in a handbasket, Ray?"

"Beats me."

"Remember how she was in high school? Charming? Seductive? Center of everything?"

"I do remember," I told him, thinking about the young Belle who sashayed around school as if she was the prettiest thing God ever created, and most of us agreed with her.

Blake shook his head and seemed to recover. He picked up a bottle of cleaner and sprayed his workbench, using a clean cloth to wipe the surface. When he finished, he slid off his stool and walked to the door to get a view of the house. He stood there running his hand over his short gray hair.

"Looks like those church ladies are still in the kitchen. I think I'll pressure-wash the back buildings. Pretty sure I saw some mud daubers taking up nesting under the eaves."

I had to appreciate the man's uncanny knack for finding unnecessary work to occupy himself with when he was determined to avoid something unpleasant, like a kitchen full of church ladies. Before he got away, I had to ask the kind of questions you hate to ask someone in a world of hurt but know you've got to. I tried to lay a little padding on the skids so it wouldn't sound so tough.

"After you've had time to get over the shock, we'll need to talk about Miss Belle's legal affairs, for the record," I told him, doing my dead level best to sound more matter of fact than I felt.

"What kind of affairs?"

"Wills and such."

"Okay. No problem," he answered. "I have files in the house. Let me know what you need."

I tried not to let out the big sigh of relief I was holding in. One more question and I was done for now.

"When we were out there in the field you said you knew we were looking into the possibility someone may have killed your wife. So, you understand why I have to ask. Do you know of anyone who would want to do her harm?"

"Ray, you've known Belle and me since high school. I figure you know about everything I know."

What we both knew for sure was that Belle was acquainted with everyone in town but few of them called her a friend.

"I understand but I need you to give it some serious thought. I'll call you."

He nodded and headed for the back.

Three down. Four to go.

CHAPTER 8

I knocked as softly as I could. "Miss Lilly, it's Ray. You got a minute?"

When the door opened, I was pretty near nose-to-nose with Ed McCombs. He signaled me to be quiet and stepped into the hallway, easing the door shut behind him.

"She's finally closed her eyes. I think she'll sleep for a bit," Ed said in a hushed voice.

"I didn't know you were here."

"Couldn't leave her alone, now, could I?"

"I'm going to need to talk to Miss Lilly."

"Can't it wait?"

I decided to call an audible. Ed was on my short list of suspects, so I figured I'd talk to him first and catch Miss Lilly after her nap. Ed had been keeping company with Miss Lilly since he moved in with his Uncle Buster following two hard tours of duty with the Marines in Afghanistan.

Miss Molly Ivins, flat-out one of the funniest women ever to write for a Texas newspaper, once said that you could gauge how deep you were in the South by how many dogs died when the porch collapsed. Miss Molly's description is a perfect fit for Buster McCombs' place, across the road from where I stood. Most days Ed stays busier than a one-legged man at an ass-kicking contest earning enough cash to pay the taxes and stay on top of repairs. He'll rake together enough to pay for a broken well pump only to find the roofer did such a shoddy job after the last storm that there's mold under the tin and the whole thing must be torn off and redone.

Ed hadn't yet celebrated his thirty-fifth birthday but his combat tours in the bloody Korangal Valley had aged him. Since returning to Texas, he'd let his hair grow and the deep creases and blotchy patches on his skin told the story of hours under the unforgiving Texas sun. But the toll was more than haircuts and sunburns. Ed wore his combat experience in a cold, empty space behind his eyes. It was as if something evil had taken up residence in there. Even in happy moments it managed to cast an endless gray haze over the carefree young recruit who'd signed up to serve after 9-11. Even though he still carried himself with a soldierly bearing, you could feel the weight of whatever had happened over there dragging behind him like a heavy chain.

I remember the day Ed met Miss Lilly. It was just a few days after he moved in with Buster. R.W. was helping Ed mend the fence that separated Buster's place from the highway. I had just pulled over to unload some tools I offered to loan Ed when Miss Lilly, walking along the road, stopped to watch.

"Why don't you boys just tear down that sorry excuse for a fence? Doesn't look like it's worth the wire and sweat it'll take to fix," she said, holding her hat high over her head to shade her face.

Ed, who'd had his back to the road, turned around when he heard her, got one look at those extraordinary eyes, and dropped a hammer on his foot. R.W. started laughing and introduced the two of them. For her part, Miss Lilly, who'd grown used to town folks gossiping behind her back because she was still single past her thirtieth birthday, had that look of someone who'd just found something they hadn't even known they'd lost. She reached down, picked up the hammer, and rolled up her sleeves.

"If you're hell bent on fixing it, suppose the neighborly thing to do would be to pitch in," she said. The three of them spent the day working in the sun and the evening cooling off over pitchers of beer.

Miss Belle made it clear in loud and unflattering language that Ed was never going to be good enough for her daughter. She offered her opinion to anyone in town who would take the time to listen. Miss Lilly knew that someday she would have to choose between love for Ed and loyalty to her mother since there would never be room for both. A suspicious pitcher of orange juice appeared to have made the choice for Miss Lilly and for Ed.

That's what brought me to Miss Lilly's door with a boatload of questions. Since I had some of the same questions for Ed, I didn't mind that he stood in the way of my plans to interview Miss Lilly.

"No problem, Ed. I understand. I need to talk to you, too. Let's get it out of the way while she's resting," I told him motioning toward the staircase.

"It's probably better if we talk up here."

I figured he was right since the kitchen was still overrun with church ladies. We walked down the hall to one of Miss Belle's fancy guest rooms. It faced the rear of the house overlooking the heavy rose trellis that framed most of the back porch. Since the window was open it was easy to hear the church ladies' cackle coming up from the kitchen below.

"Trouble with Miss Belle is that she had everything she wanted and what she had she didn't want," we heard one of them say.

"Poor Blake. She kept him on a short leash. Maybe now he'll get to travel some," another chimed in.

The guest bedroom was chock full of antebellum doodads Miss Belle was prone to collecting at flea markets. I settled for an odd-looking chair with flaming red silk upholstery and carved roses framing the backrest. It was the kind of chair that made you feel as if someone was waiting to whop you on the head with a stick if you didn't sit up straight.

After looking around, Ed elected to stand next to the open window. I don't know if it was his Army training to protect your flank or an unwillingness to subject his six-foot frame to sitting on one of the prissy chairs. I couldn't blame him one bit for his choice. I was wishing I'd made the same decision since my knees were practically in my chest.

"Miss Lilly told the DPS she was in Austin yesterday," I said.

"That's right," Ed replied.

"Were you in Austin, too?"

"I was."

"Were you together?"

"I don't know what you mean."

I could see how this was going to go. He was playing it tight-lipped, and I had no time for *Twenty Questions*. I was about to tell him that when Miss Lilly opened the door and joined us.

She had a quilt wrapped around her shoulders. Since her feet were bare you couldn't miss the rose tattoo on her right ankle. Katie Brooks, who seems to know all the gossip in town, once told me the story of the rose tattoo. It was the usual high school rebellion. Miss Lilly and R.W. slipped away to Austin on prom night. She got the dainty rose on her ankle and he had thorns tattooed around his bicep.

To say it didn't sit well with Miss Belle would be an understatement. She called the tattoos vulgar and banned Miss Lilly from the house for a month. The girl was to sleep over at the Seville place. It was one of the rare times Blake interfered with Belle's parenting decisions and put his foot down, bringing Lilly home after one night. Belle never forgave either one of them.

Lilly curled up on a camelback Victorian sofa near the fireplace and Ed joined her, wrapping his arms around her.

"I thought you were going to rest," Ed said to her in a soft voice as if talking to a sleepy child.

"Go ahead and tell him, Ed," Lilly answered. "We don't have anything to hide. We went down yesterday and spent the night at the Driskill. I'm not ashamed of it."

"He doesn't have any right to bother you with personal questions at a time like this," Ed said, giving me the snake eye.

"Someone killed her, Ed. The Sheriff's got to ask questions. Right, Ray?"

"Yes, ma'am."

"Shoot."

"Let's start with your trip to Austin."

"We were there for the quarterly meeting of the Texas Free Range Cattlemen's Association," Ed said.

"Believe me, you haven't lived a complete life until you've sat through reports from the Texas Animal Health Commission on the latest breakthroughs in brucellosis prevention and treatment and a sure enough droop-your-eyeballs discussion about plans by the USDA to improve country-of-origin labeling of meat products," Lilly added with a slight groan.

"Who else was at the meeting?" I asked.

"I was there because my Uncle Buster couldn't make it. Some of the information is important. Bobby Seville and Lilly's dad, Blake, are both Directors so, of course, they had to go down for the morning Board meeting," Ed answered.

"Daddy always asks me to go and I don't mind getting out of Lantz," Lilly added.

I asked Lilly to walk me through the day. She explained that the Board meets in the morning. The Association holds its quarterly conferences at the iconic Driskill Hotel, built by one of Texas's original cattle barons in the 1860s in downtown Austin. The Board agenda covers things like budget, personnel matters, pending litigation, and lobbying.

"All the fellas on the Board have egos as big as their opinions, so they shut the door and fight it out," she said.

"Did you see your mother before you left?" I asked.

"You cut right to it, don't you? Like I said, Daddy left early. Mama was still in bed so I looked in on her and told her I'd see her when I got back from Austin. I had a few chores. Hattie was downstairs. We had breakfast and talked. I was packed so after I finished my chores, I loaded up and drove to Austin. Ed and I drove down separately."

I looked at Ed and he answered my unspoken question. "I had to put in some hours at work, so I didn't get to Austin until around noon. Lilly had already checked in at the Driskill."

Lilly said that she likes to use the hotel's spa facilities and relax before the meeting.

"The hotel can confirm all of this. Both of us were there in time for the noon buffet and the afternoon events," she said.

She explained that's when several hundred Association members from across Texas congregate for a big beef buffet, speeches, and informational presentations. The whole shebang ends with a reception at around five in the afternoon. Some members leave early. Most, however, stay overnight to party on Sixth Street, the center of the Capital City's restaurant and music district.

"Did you hook up with your father and Bobby Seville?" I asked.

Lilly and Ed made eye contact, but neither gave a quick answer.

"I think Bobby may have left early. I didn't see him after lunch. Of course, I may have missed him," Ed finally said.

"What about you, Miss Lilly?"

"Same here. Ed and I noticed because we usually meet up and at least have a drink together."

"What about your father?"

"I know for sure he was there at about three o'clock," Lilly said. "A speaker who was yakking on and on about estate planning had nearly put me to sleep so I almost jumped out of my skin when Daddy tapped on my shoulder. He was excited and wanted to know what I thought about her ideas. He said I should take notes because she had some interesting ideas on inheritance taxes and Texas homestead exemptions and such designed to protect debtors."

"What happened after the presentation?"

"I told Daddy I was going to spend the night. He said he might have to leave Austin early. That's why we agreed to meet at the Store this morning."

Lilly said the Association reception could sometimes turn into a bacchanal.

"After a lunch of beef served every which way, we decided some seafood would hit the spot," she said. "We ate at Eddie V's, hung around Sixth Street, and then ended up at the Parker Jazz Club."

"Anything else?"

They gave each other that look again.

"Walking back to the Driskill I saw R.W. talking to a couple of fellas on the street. I waved, but I don't think he saw me," Ed said.

"What time was that?"

"Can't be sure but I'd say about seven."

The gaggle of church ladies on the porch below was growing louder. It was clear they had no idea that their voices carried. They were still talking about Miss Belle.

"You'd think butter wouldn't melt in her mouth," an anonymous voice drifted up.

"They'll be able to write her obituary by clipping paragraphs from the pages in the *Methodist Church Bulletin*," came another comment.

"You could sure count on her to embellish every story and repeat every secret," a third voice offered.

Miss Lilly jumped up and ran to the open window.

"Hey, bitches, why don't you get your sorry asses off my Mama's porch."

I would have given anything to see the scramble below. You could hear the shuffle of feet and quick goodbyes as the women made their exit. I couldn't help but wonder how the scene would play out at the next Ladies' Auxiliary meeting.

When she sat back down, Miss Lilly was fuming.

"What else do you have to ask me?"

I made a show of flipping through my notes and jotting down a few check marks, not because it was necessary. I wanted to give Miss Lilly time to cool off. I may have mentioned Miss Lilly intimidates me a bit, so I wasn't quite ready to take her on. Ed came to my rescue by explaining he needed to go to work. I told him I would catch up with him later. He gave Miss Lilly a goodbye hug, whispering something in her ear before leaving.

Alone with Miss Lilly I played at my note-checking charade. Then she asked me a question. It nearly broke my heart.

"She didn't have a lot of friends, did she?"

"I wouldn't say that."

"You heard those women. She worked with them every week at the church, yet they had nothing good to say."

"No sense putting much stock in what those old busybodies said. Waste of time."

"Do you think she knew?"

"You're in a better position to answer that than I am."

"Course she did. She wasn't stupid," Lilly muttered, more to herself than to me.

Lilly pulled the quilt around her shoulders and hugged herself with it, tucking it around her feet. As she did her toe got caught in a piece that was worn and frayed. She began to pick at the fabric.

"My Gammy Tackett made this quilt. Mama didn't like it because it was nearly worn out. That's what I liked about it. It reminded me of how life is, you know?"

"How so?"

"Gammy said you can't always choose what life throws at you. If you put your mind to it though, you can take the scraps and you can sew them up and make something of them. Even the thinnest piece of goods, all faded with too much washing, can be crisp and shiny again if you apply some starch and steam and darn up the holes, or you can sew pieces into something useful, like this quilt. With skill and a good steam iron, you can bring life back to the faded places. I want to believe Gammy is right and life is that way, too."

She kept picking at the hole in the quilt and then looked up at me, her eyes moist and pleading.

"Do you have any idea of who might have killed my Mama?"

"Actually, I was going to ask you that very question."

Before she could answer, Hattie opened the door and looked at me.

"When you're finished bothering Miss Lilly, send her on down to the kitchen. I'm warming up some of the food the church ladies left. If she comes down, I think between the two of us we can get her daddy to eat something," Hattie said. "Will you be joining us, Sheriff?"

I thanked Hattie but told her I was done.

"For now."

CHAPTER 9

I could hear the wail of a clarinet as I got to Sara's front porch. She'd cranked up the speakers on her turntable for *Rhapsody in Blue*. She must have seen me drive up because she yelled from inside before I could knock.

"It's not locked, Ray. Come on in."

Fifteen pounds of Maine Coon cut in front of me when I stepped inside. Sara had rescued a raven-haired kitten from the animal shelter and named the cute ball of fur "Twizy," after the tiny French car that is little more than a motorcycle with a roof and windows. Three years later there was nothing even remotely reminiscent of that rescue kitten in the shaggy, oversized Hell Cat that shot in front of me as I stepped into Sara's place.

Hell Cat, my name for Twizy, caused dogs to whimper and scurry away with their tails tucked between their legs. Sara's friends bore scars on their arms and legs where Hell Cat had drawn blood. Sara posted a sign on the door warning visitors not to try to pet Twizy. Like I said, Hell Cat.

Sara was settled into the curve of a couch that I'd helped her rescue from an old barn. The room, like Sara, was lived in rather than buttoned up; assembled rather than decorated with intention. The pillows piled around her in a comfortable way signaled this was her special spot. The pillow she propped her arm on was imprinted with a faded Arthur Miller quote: "Maybe all one can do is hope to end up with the right regrets."

My Sweet Wife once told me Sara reminded her of an unmade bed. I got her point as Sara reached through the neck of her shirt and adjusted her bra strap and then used her fingers to comb a patch of undisciplined hair out of her eyes.

"Join me?" she asked, indicating her glass of whiskey.

"I'm good," I said.

"It's been one of those," Sara said, taking another sip. "Mama's under the weather, again."

I didn't respond because I was searching for a place to sit since Hell Cat was now splayed out across the only available chair close to Sara. I reached to clear the cantankerous feline away and she rewarded me with a deep scratch on my right hand. I let go of her and she leaped to the floor, her yellow eyes on me in a fixed, menacing gaze, pawing the rug as she backed away emitting a sound halfway between a growl and ghostly howl.

"Don't let Twizy get to you, Ray," Sara said. "It's her way."

"Can't see why you put up with that animal," I said, sucking on my wound and settling into the seat.

"Did you ever watch Star Trek? The female Klingons had an aggressive way of showing affection. It's the same with Twizy. When she draws blood, I think of it as her version of a Klingon love ritual," Sara said.

I took out my notepad, flipping to an empty page. Before I asked my first question, I noticed Sara had closed her eyes was lost in the music.

"When I play that record, I think of my G-ma," she said.

Sara had something on her mind, so I waited for the story, keeping Hell Cat in my peripheral vision. After another sip of whiskey, Sara delivered.

"I was around twelve and we were all crowded into a two-bedroom unit out at Cross Timbers Courts. The place was in such bad shape that every few days I had to crawl under the bed in my room with scissors to trim the grass that had grown up through the cracks in the concrete floor."

I didn't want to interrupt Sara's story or I would have mentioned that the city finally condemned the Courts and torn them down a few years back. Her eyes were still closed and she was lost in remembering.

"My tennis shoes were frayed and full of holes, and the rubber in the back was flopping loose. I really needed new ones. G-ma saved up nickels and dimes from her night shift waiting tables and sent me to Kelley's Dry Goods in Georgetown to get a new pair before school started. I had a pocket full of coins rattling in my jeans when I walked by the open door of the music store. That was the first time I heard that sweet, sweet sound."

Sara opened her eyes and took another sip of whiskey.

"You know what that's like, don't you, Ray? To want something so bad, you do what you have to do to get it?"

"I guess."

"I bought that record right there and then. Had to use duct tape on my shoes before the school year was over. You know, I wore out four or five pairs of tennis shoes before I graduated high school, and yet I've still got my Gershwin."

Sara polished off her drink, using her tongue to lick the last of the whiskey off the ice cube. She set the glass down and got up, turning her back to me.

"What do you think is the best cure for what ails you, Ray? Stop drinking all together or really lay into the hooch and drink until you don't feel it anymore?"

She didn't wait for an answer. I suspect she didn't want one. She turned off the record player and gave the vinyl a gentle wipe with a soft cloth before sliding it back into its cover and returning it with care to a slot in her collection on a shelf below the player. When she turned back to face me, she looked tired and somehow older. She sat back down on the couch, again building a pillow fort around her, clasping her hands together over her knees, and leaning in toward me.

"You didn't come here to listen to stories about my sad little life, did you, Ray? You came here to talk about who killed Belle."

"What makes you say that?"

"I'm not a fool, Ray. News in this sorry excuse for a town travels faster than shit out of a goose. You've been making the rounds and you wouldn't do that if she'd died in her sleep or if she'd done the first decent thing in her life and ended our collective misery by killing herself. Someone got tired of putting up with her crap and killed the First Lady of Lantz. Now you're stuck with the thankless task of figuring out who did the deed. Problem is you have a town full of suspects. Am I right?"

Before I could answer, Grace Lawrence shuffled in from the hallway, leaning heavily on her walker. The old woman was more skeleton-like than the last time I'd seen her and what hair remained on her head was in tiny gray clumps that left a lot of pink scalp exposed. I'm not sure she saw me. Her housecoat hung open and she wasn't wearing much underneath.

"Sara Baby, Mama needs to pee."

Sara was at her mother's side almost before I could, out of respect, divert my gaze.

I made the mistake of forgetting about Hell Cat. The second Sara and her mama were out of sight, the beast was in my lap using my torso for a scratching post. The last thing I needed today was cat hair on my khaki britches. I dumped the chickenshit on the floor and made a beeline out the door.

Under different circumstances I would spend a minute telling you about my sordid history with the feline of the species. All that needs to be said for now is the presence of Sara's yellow-eyed demon was a big part of my motivation to delay the interrogation. It turned out to be a good thing.

I called out to Sara that I'd be back later as I made my strategic exit. When I got to my patrol car, Katie Sue Brooks from my office was broadcasting repeatedly over the police radio, trying to get my attention. She does that a lot.

"Sheriff Ray, you there? What is your 10-20?"

"It's me, Katie. What's happening?"

"Can you take a 10-61?" she asked. I could hear her shuffling papers in the background.

"For the love of God, what are you talking about?"

For reasons I could not figure out, she answered in a low voice. "A 10-61 is a sensitive message, Boss."

"Where are you getting all of this?"

"Google!"

"Well, Google this: I don't have time for any more of your coded talk. Tell me straight up what you called me about."

I could hear her chuckling. She knew I wasn't really upset. We both appreciated how lucky I was to have her running the office.

"Phil Ashworth over in Austin wants you to call him. Sounded important."

"Will do."

"Over and out," she giggled.

"Hold on. Have you heard from Johnnie?"

"Do you mean Deputy Lake?"

"Who else do we know who is named Johnnie?"

"No sir, I have not heard from Deputy Lake since this morning."

"See if you can locate that sorry so-and-so."

"Will do," she said. Her answer sounded like a salute.

Just to be ornery, I said, "WD-40," before I hung up.

I used my mobile phone to call Phil. He answered right away. After a bit of the usual small talk about the total lack of measurable precipitation in our rain gauges and what have you, he got to the police business that was the purpose of his call. It was a humdinger.

The medical examiner had finished a preliminary examination of Veda Tackett and concluded that the cause of death was not poison the way we originally thought. Rather she'd likely died from asphyxiation. You might imagine it took me a minute or two to get my head around this bombshell.

They'd found an insulated cable wire wrapped around her neck. Seems the crusty patch in the orange juice pitcher was more than likely a powerful sedative. It had knocked her out but was not what killed her. After she was unconscious, someone strangled her with the wire. They were still analyzing the garrote. It appeared to be an eighteen-gauge wire of the type used for dog fences. None of us had noticed the wire during our initial examination at the crime scene because of all the folds of skin around Miss Belle's plump neck. Her lacy nightgown and her fancy sleep jacket completed the camouflage.

"I'll be damned."

CHAPTER 10

I've never known anyone who was as comfortable in his own skin as Robert Wayne "Bobby" Seville. In high school he made a sport out of spooking folks, especially the girls, by shining a black light on the implant that replaced the front tooth he lost during a football scrimmage, because it glowed green in the dark. When his hairline started to back away from his forehead, he got the barber to clip what remained close to the scalp. He told folks that he figured God covered up the heads he was ashamed of. Even though he was rich as Croesus, he was the first to roll up his sleeves and pitch in if someone needed help. Like the saying goes, if the table is wobbling you could count on Bobby to show up with a shim.

As I may have mentioned, Bobby could talk the hinges off a gate. For him there was always a story to be told, or made up, and he wasn't bothered one bit if it reflected poorly on him. I've lost count of how many times he told the one of how he met Monica on that fraternity field trip to D.C. He was waiting in the hallway to meet his Congressman. She was talking to co-workers from the office next door. She was from a charming colonial town in a nearby Maryland county, close enough that she could take the

Metro subway line to work every day. To his Texas ear the lilt in the way she spoke sounded exotic, so he mistook it for a foreign accent and he assumed she was from overseas.

He was smitten in a heartbeat.

"Where you from, Miss Blue Eyes?" he asked her.

"Thurmont."

"Well, I'm from Texas," he said, giving her a tip of his cowboy hat. "Have you heard of Texas?"

"Why yes, sir, I believe I have."

"How do you like the U.S. of A. up till now?" he asked, giving her his best shit-eating grin.

In light of an ignorant comment like that some women might have given him a smartass reply. Not Monica. She was all in for the game.

"So far, so good. How about you?"

Bobby failed to take the hint when he noticed her girlfriends giggling.

"Well, darling, I don't think much of D.C., but I must admit that you do a lot to improve things," he said holding out his hand for a shake. "My name's Bobby Wayne Seville. What's yours?"

Before Monica could answer, Bobby's fraternity brothers called out that they were ready for him in the Congressman's office and he rushed to join them. Thirty minutes later he was back at the Maryland Congressman's office, hat in hand. He'd been given a quick geography lesson by the staff in the adjoining office and was feeling like a proper fool. That's what he'd come to tell Monica.

"I don't think you're a fool," she told him. "I think you're cute."

That's all Bobby needed by way of encouragement. Three weeks later they were married. Bobby kept on telling that story long after Monica died.

There was no shortage of Monica stories where Bobby was concerned. No matter where a conversation started, something always seemed to put him in mind of a Monica story. He'd tell people about how she'd taught him to free the sweetest bits of meat from crab claws by hitting them "just so" with a tiny wooden hammer. He loved repeating the one about the flour fight they had in the kitchen when he showed her how to make scratch biscuits. Before it was over, they'd emptied an entire bag of White Lily on each other. Since the ceiling fans were spinning above them, it took weeks to get the flour out of the crevices in the baseboards.

She gave him a hard time about how Texas cooks fried everything, including vegetables. He fought back by introducing her to Tex-Mex, cornbread with sweet milk, chili cook-offs, barbeque ribs, and boiled shrimp with red sauce spiked with so much horseradish that it made her eyes water. She bragged about the Chesapeake Bay until he took her to South Padre Island. She ached for the Appalachian Mountains back home, so he packed up and drove for ten hours to the Davis Mountains and then on to the Big Bend. She fell for Texas wildflowers, so their ritual was to drive the Willow City Loop every spring to catch Indian paintbrush and bluebonnets banking around every turn.

The way his eyes would tear up when he talked about Monica kept you from complaining. With cancer taking Monica so fast when R.W. was only three, folks knew that Bobby's stories helped fill the empty places. That's why we let him talk the way only Bobby could talk.

There was one story that I didn't hear from him. I'd hoped to God he didn't know it. It was about Monica's ashes and Miss Belle.

When Monica realized that the chemo wasn't working, she made Bobby swear to cremate her and scatter her ashes at Cunningham Falls near her hometown. The Falls cascade down the Catoctin Mountain for miles, forming shallow pools in some places and steep drops in others. Monica and Bobby were married at a spot where a boulder splits the falls into two channels. The waters join back together into one clear stream a little further down the mountain. She had this romantic idea that it symbolized that even when she was gone from him for a time, someday they would come together again in the same way that the stream split and then reunited. Monica told Bobby that if he spread her ashes on that spot, she would wait for him there until he joined her again, nourishing the rich mountain soil with her remains, helping flowers to bloom.

He swore he would do it. After she was gone, time slipped away. Years later Monica's ashes still rested in a china urn on his mantel while he raised his baby boy and grieved. The urn was navy blue with gold and yellow dots that he said represented lightning bugs. Bobby told me that he had it specially made because Monica was like a firefly in the night, burning bright but only there for a moment. Here, then gone. We all figured that Bobby put off the trip to Maryland because he couldn't bear to let even a little bit of Monica go. He wanted to keep every grain of her to himself.

The Ladies' Auxiliary at the First United Methodist Church rallied around Bobby when Monica passed, making sure the young widower and his boy had plenty of home-cooked meals. Miss Belle fell into the habit of bringing over noodle casserole and pecan pie every other Wednesday before church services. She'd fuss around in Bobby's kitchen, organizing the cutlery and rearranging the pantry. Bobby allowed as how her pie was so full of butter, corn syrup, and cholesterol-packed pecans that the boys down at the General Store nicknamed the recipe a "heart attack in a pie shell."

Miss Belle laughed with him, offering tips about laundry and unsolicited opinions about child raising. She'd bring little presents for R.W., sing to the toddler, and let him cuddle on her lap. It wasn't long before R.W. grew attached to Miss Belle. Often as not she'd take the child home with her to spend the night with Lilly. Over the years Miss Lilly and R.W. grew up like brother and sister.

The story about the stunt Miss Belle had pulled at the start of Lent involving the contents of Bobby's special lightning bug urn had only recently reached me. S.W. had first heard the story via the Ladies' Auxiliary grapevine following the annual bake sale.

I decided to go over the particulars with my Sweet Wife one more time to make sure I had the details clear in my mind before I talked to Bobby. That's one reason I made a quick detour by the house before stopping at the Seville ranch. In addition, S.W. needed to hear it straight from me why I wouldn't be home for supper. I'd arranged with Phil to fill him in on my interviews and I wanted to get his notes on what the DPS had uncovered. Since the Seville place was on the road to Austin, it made sense to stop by and talk to Bobby on the way out of town. He was the last interview on my list. Six down. One to go.

Driving home I thought back when S.W. first came home all abuzz with the story about Miss Belle and Monica's ashes. She said everyone in the Ladies' Auxiliary agreed on how Miss Belle came to steal the ashes and what she did with them. Certain other key parts of the story were, however, in dispute. Miss Belle was ready with a baggie and a spoon when Bobby went out to the barn. The deed was done as quick as a sailor's wink.

"What would cause her to do such a thing?" I asked.

"That's the problem. Miss Belle either told different versions of the story to different people or, in the repeating of the story, it was altered and embellished," S.W. explained.

"Some say she was mad at Bobby because he turned her down flat when she made a pass at him. Some say it was the other way around," my wife explained. "Some say Belle was only being contrary. She'd been listening to Bobby go on and on for years about 'Monica-this' and 'Monica-that' to the point that she wanted have a bit of fun at Saint Monica's expense."

I didn't say anything because I didn't want to interrupt S.W.'s chain of thought.

"Some say the whole thing had nothing to do with Monica or with Bobby. They claim Belle was mad at the new Methodist preacher because he refused to listen to her advice. She called him 'uppity' and wanted to bring him down a peg or two. With Belle you might believe almost anything."

"Or everything," I said. "What did she do with the ashes?"

"Like I said it was Wednesday. Ash Wednesday."

My Sweet Wife laid it all out. Miss Belle was on the Altar Committee setting up for Ash Wednesday services. It was easy to mix a scoop of Monica in with the burned palm leaves when no one was looking.

"I can practically picture her self-satisfied snickering as the preacher smeared oily Monica-ash-laced crosses on the forehead of all the fine Methodists who came to services," S.W. said, shaking her head.

"Jesus."

"Exactly."

What was peculiar, S.W. explained, was how Miss Belle kept the whole affair to herself until right after the bake sale. Then, for reasons that are not at all clear, Miss Belle began to share the story of her escapade around. It didn't take long before the Ladies' Auxiliary grapevine was buzzing with nothing other than Miss Belle's Ash Wednesday shenanigans.

When I heard the story the first time, I did a little research to see if desecration of remains might be a crime. I didn't find much and lost interest. Until Miss Belle died.

I got home a little after three o'clock and found S.W. making 7-Up biscuits. It was enough to make me want to change my plans about the trip to Austin. But duty called. I gave her a quick report on what had happened during the day and my plans to meet with Phil.

"Before I interview Bobby, I need you to help me with something," I told her. "Do you think Bobby knew about what Miss Belle did on Ash Wednesday?"

"In this town? If you tell one person you may as well take out an ad in the weekly. I can't say for sure. It wouldn't surprise me one little bit if someone told him."

I leaned in to kiss her goodbye when I thought of one final question. "Did anyone come up with an explanation on why Miss Belle would keep what she did with Monica's ashes a secret and then suddenly start talking about it?"

"No way to ask her now, is there?"

CHAPTER 11

What got into Miss Belle to suddenly start talking about her little stunt with Monica's ashes? If, when, and how did Bobby find out about it? How did he react to Belle's blatant disrespect of his beloved wife? Was it enough to drive him to revenge?

I was still chewing on those questions as I rattled across the cattle guard at the entrance to Bobby's place. Bobby's stockade fence is made of the finest redwood slats and runs for three and a half miles on either side of his custom-made steel archway entrance. The archway itself consists of two tall T's holding up a Lone Star that together frame the beginning of a gravel driveway that twists through the pasture about a quarter mile to his rambling ranch house and assorted outbuildings.

Bobby was riding up in the rear with several workmen when he spotted me. He took off his hat and used it to wave. I parked around back of the house and watched as Bobby jumped down from the saddle and turned his horse over to one of his crew. I stayed with my car while Bobby shared a laugh with the fellas before heading my way, using his hat to slap the dust from his jeans.

"Been expecting you, Ray. Do you want some iced tea or, maybe, a beer?"

"Tea's fine. Sweet."

I'm not the kind who is prone to break the Tenth Commandment, but it's almost impossible not to covet when you're invited to sit a spell on Bobby's screened porch. It stretches the full length of the back side of his house with ceiling fans every few feet. It's the kind of place were a man can play a round of dominos or eat a mess of fried catfish without feeling crowded.

When Bobby opened the door to fetch the iced tea, the sound of his television blasted out from the kitchen. Bobby made it a habit to turn the sound way up first thing when he got out of bed in the morning and kept it going until he tucked in at night. He says it drowns out the sounds that aren't there anymore. Sounds such as Monica talking on the phone, Monica calling his name, Monica rattling around in the kitchen, whistling.

Mostly it covers up the missing sound of Monica singing, the way she did, off-key and loud when she thought she was alone. It was so tone-deaf that when she was in church, she would pretend to sing along by mouthing the hymns. If Bobby heard her singing in the next room, he would tiptoe close to the door to eavesdrop because he knew she would stop if she thought someone was listening. She once told Bobby she hoped that when she got to heaven, they would let her sing real loud. These days Bobby used the TV volume to cover up the fact that Monica's God-awful singing wasn't filling the kitchen anymore.

When he returned to the porch with two quart-size glasses of tea, Bobby used his foot to close the door behind him.

"Think that's enough," I teased, wrapping both hands around the huge glass as I accepted it from Bobby.

"Should hold us for a while," Bobby said.

As he settled into the chair across from me, I pointed out the three Mason jars that I'd brought from home. My Sweet Wife believes you can pickle anything if you combine the perfect spices and correct vinegar. She had long since graduated from watermelon rind, carrots, peppers, and okra to more experimental veggies. Bobby shared her passion and she kept him well supplied.

"That would be your eggplant, your asparagus, and your green beans," I told Bobby as I pointed to each jar.

"You are one lucky man, Ray C. Tell her we'll go into business when she's ready."

"She's working her heart out looking for the perfect brine for Cherry Belle radishes."

"I can't wait," Bobby grinned, rubbing his hands together and licking his lips.

After a long drink of ice-cold tea, Bobby asked. "How's Blake holding up?"

"You were there this morning."

"I hear that they think Belle was killed by poison," he said.

"Where did you hear that?"

"Let's see. Hattie hinted about it when we were at the Tackett place. R.W. heard it from Miss Lilly. Then at least four church ladies were called to share rumors. What can I say? You know Lantz."

"I guess I do."

"What do the DPS folks think?"

"Too early to say. I'm on my way to meet up with them."

"And you needed to interview me first."

I pulled out my notebook and pen.

"Tell me about yesterday."

Bobby took another drink and his face relaxed into a smile. I knew not to read anything into it since he was the kind of man whose face just naturally rests into a smile, even when he was all by himself.

"Blake and I had to be in Austin early for the Cattlemen's Association Board meeting. I considered going in Saturday night and sleeping over because I like the sky first thing in the morning when the sun is coming up over the lake and the skyline is lit up. Monica said old timers used to call Austin the City of the Violet Crown. They say that comes from the writer O. Henry. She was sure she could see a purple haze in the hills when the light aligns just a certain way early of a morning. I don't get it, but I pretend that I do. Besides, traffic on the interstate is pretty near tolerable early in the day."

"But you waited and went in Sunday morning early."

"That's right."

"I understand the Board meeting was over around noon."

"That's right. We had speakers and such for the full membership after lunch."

"What was on the agenda?"

"Why don't I send you a printout of the program? It has all the details."

"That would be helpful."

"The most fired up the membership got was during a presentation by this guy from the federal government talking about plans for a big ol' fence along the Mexican border. There was near riot when an old codger interrupted the speaker and called him a name I'll not repeat here. Told him he was making the same mistake as the French who built the Maginot Line after W-W-One. They believed an expensive wall of weapons and enforcements could keep the Germans out. 'Didn't work then, won't work now,' he yelled. The speaker broke into a flop sweat, and everyone in the audience started calling each other out."

"Sorry I missed it."

, people have strong feelings about. What with ..inent domain to build the darn thing, my guess is ..awyers are going to be the only winners," Bobby said. ..ce things settled down, the poor speaker had to reboot his computer because his presentation shut down."

I took a minute for a long drink of tea before hitting him with my next question. "Did R.W. go down with you?"

For just a blink, I think my question caught Bobby off guard.

"No. I drove down alone."

"What time did things finish up?"

"I'm going to say the formal part of the meeting ended some-time around five. Don't hold me to it. It's all in the program."

"When did R.W. get home?"

"Couldn't say. You know kids."

I flipped through my notebook, sipped some tea, and tapped my pen on the table. I was trying to figure out how to ask Bobby about Monica's ashes without being too direct. I shouldn't have worried.

"I don't envy you the job of trying to figure out if someone killed Miss Belle. She had a way of getting under a lotta folks' skin."

"Even you?"

Bobby finished off his iced tea and asked if I needed a refill. I knew better than to fill up with caffeine because I still faced a sixty-mile highway drive to Austin. I was under the impression he was taking his time before he answered.

"What can I say? She was good to R.W. After Monica passed, Belle was always around to help me take care of the boy when I was grieving so."

"That's not really an answer to the question now, is it?"

Bobby got up and walked to the screen door, looking out across the back pasture where his men were tending to horses.

"In those early days when R.W. was a baby, I was lost. When he got a fever or scraped his knee, she was tender with him. I could teach him to ride a horse and dig a post hole, but, a little boy needs a woman's touch."

Bobby came back and sat down, picking up his iced tea but holding it in his hand without taking a drink.

"The boy means everything to me, but to tell you the truth I never really understood him. He had the oddest ideas. When he was eleven, he asked me if we could hang the Christmas tree upside down from the ceiling. I ask you, where does a boy get a notion like that?"

I was at a loss but lamely suggested that maybe he got it from watching too much TV.

"Maybe you're right. Seems he had a different way of looking at the world. Like the time we were putting together one of those puzzles that's a map of the United States. He mastered it so fast that he was bored so I gave him a *World Atlas*. One day he showed me the Colorado puzzle piece and told me that he'd been comparing it to the topographical map in the atlas. He said if you looked straight down at the puzzle piece from above, you'd think the state was little more than a box. All ninety-degree angles and straight lines. If you could look at it from the side like in the atlas, you can see the outline of the mountains and prairies. From that way, Colorado has a truly interesting profile."

"I guess he was saying that it's all in the way you look at things."

"That's my point exactly. I think he is smarter than he lets on. He sees things in a way that I can't."

"That's a good thing, ain't it?"

"Not if you hide it. I get the feeling he's ashamed of who he is and is running away from his smarts. It's like he is two people. The one he thinks I want him to be and one he keeps covered up because he believes I'd have trouble understanding. One boy on the outside. A different boy on the inside. I don't know how to tell him that I love him any old way. Do you know what I'm trying to say?"

To be honest I wasn't for sure. That's why I gave him the answer I thought he wanted.

"Sure. I understand."

He noticed that my iced tea glass was empty and again offered to refill it.

"No thanks. Like I said, I have a road trip coming up. You were telling me about Miss Belle."

"Sorry about that. My point is that Belle encouraged that kind of thing in R.W. All those old movies and such. He liked hanging out with her. I appreciated it when he was a baby. As he got older, I worried that maybe I made a mistake not being more involved with him. You know?"

"Do you think this has something to do with how Miss Belle died?"

"Hell, no. I was only trying to explain why I've always been forgiving-and-forgetting when it came to Belle and her mischief, the way she treated people sometimes. She was good to R.W. and I owed her for that. You know me, Ray. Mostly I'm live-and-let-live. Yet, there comes a time . . ." his voice trailed off.

"So, you're saying you did have a bone to pick with Miss Belle."

"Lantz is a tiny town. I figure it's not worth the salt to season your fries to get tangled up in local feuds," he said. He picked up the paper napkin from under his iced tea glass. It was damp from condensation. Removing his hat, he used the napkin to wipe the sweat from his head and the inside of his hat.

"When a person keeps drawing on your good will, there comes a day when the well runs dry; a day when that person pushes you too far. Know what I mean?"

This time I was pretty sure that I knew exactly what he was talking about.

CHAPTER 12

Lantz has had its fair share of liars, con men, petty thieves, two-timers, backstabbers, and card cheats. I've personally locked up some drunks, grifters, and reprobates. Until Miss Belle was killed, we'd never had a cold-blooded killer. That's why I was glad to have backup from the Austin folk. The drive from Bobby's place to DPS Headquarters took less time than I expected. Our Lady of Perpetual Construction, the not-so-affectionate nickname for Interstate 35, was moving pretty good considering it was down to two lanes in Salado. I was looking forward to finding out what the technicians and investigators had put together.

Austin had changed since I finished my four years at The University, so I wasn't in the habit of going down there much. There's lots of ways to measure the difference between Lantz and Austin: people, traffic, food, taxes, pollution, noise, concrete, politics. For my money, the best measure is height: building height and road height. One or two houses in Arrowhead County have an upstairs and a downstairs. The old main high school over in Florence has three floors, if you count the attic. That's it. The rest of the places are flat like the roads.

In Austin they keep reaching for the sky. A-town is busting at the seams with all its pseudo-weird-dining-on-the-gravy-train-Silicon-Prairie-Music-Capitol-of-the-Universe-we're-so-Special-Willie-Nelson's-legacy that they can't build condos or stack freeway flyovers high enough to keep up with people who want a piece of the promised land and who don't mind traveling on roads that look like a sadist's idea of a concrete carnival ride. Downtown, people are stacked up like cordwood in residential towers that block out the sunlight.

Lantz, on the other hand, hasn't changed since I was a kid. Two-lane roads, churches and front porches are three things Lantz has in spades. Same six families own most everything. Lantz may be too small for a Dairy Queen, but we have the standard three-pack of Protestant righteousness that thrives in this neck of the woods: one each of the Baptist, Methodist and Church of Christ variety. Sunday morning and Wednesday evening, church parking lots spill over with folks from around the county attending worship services. Other than that, Lantz runs on the quiet side. Most of us try to be good neighbors and stay out of each other's business. One of my neighbors insists on flying the Confederate flag on a gigantic flagpole in his yard. He lives next door to an ol' boy who drives a flaming hot pink motorcycle and wears his hair in a man bun. You might say they are of a different political persuasion, but I've never heard a harsh word between them.

Five county roads meet at or near the Lantz General Store, which means the Store pretty much passes for the center of everything in town. There's not much else in the way of commerce. That is, if you don't count Cooter's knife sharpening stand that he sets up along the road on most weekends or Mrs. Petty's bait farm. Like her sign says, she sells year-round to anyone looking for "prime worms." If you want a fill up, groceries, or dry goods, you can get them in Florence or Georgetown. Over the county line you can get some pretty good beer and whiskey. For things like first rate medical care, sports, nightlife, and such, there's Austin. That list, for me anyway, now included crime-solving expertise.

The DPS Headquarters facility has all the architectural charm of a North Dallas junior high school building from the fifties, except with fewer windows. Phil was expecting me. After the usual small talk, he handed me a folder containing copies of preliminary forensic reports.

"Phew. You haven't wasted any time. How close will they be able to pinpoint the time of death?" I asked after reading the initial findings from the postmortem.

"We may get lucky because it hadn't been long since she'd eaten. Analysis of stomach contents, along with other indicators will help us narrow the TOD."

"Any sense of how long before the autopsy will be complete?"

"You can ask yourself if you'd like. Someone should be available around 4:30."

"That's okay. No need to rush. There's plenty here to work with. We just found her this morning. Have they made any decisions about the stuff in the juice pitcher?"

"I put it on the fast track. Looks like there may be more than one substance, which might explain why some of it crusted up instead of dissolving. We're testing for opioids and barbiturates as well as the usual range of suspect chemicals. The lab guys say orange juice can increase the way the body absorbs some drugs so their analysis may take a bit longer to sort out."

"Damn, man. Can I say I'm impressed?'

"We aim to please," he replied, with a quick Texas Tech "guns up" that chapped my ass. What can I say? It was good police work.

He pulled out a yellow legal pad and pen. "Your turn. What did you find out from the locals?"

"Mostly I'd say that I found out that Lantz has some mighty good liars."

"Did that surprise you?"

I decided to give him highlights of the top suspects, in order of my initial interviews.

"Young Robert Wayne Seville, Jr., known locally as R.W., says he was with Miss Belle from around three until bedtime. Says the two of them ate barbeque that he brought in from Austin while they watched old movies. Says Miss Belle was fine when he went home," I told Phil as he jotted notes.

"You doubt him?"

"Trouble is, he was spotted in Austin on Sixth Street around seven. Timing doesn't fit. Besides that, Hattie didn't find any evidence of take-out bags or used barbecue wrappers from Stubb's in the kitchen trash when she came to clean this morning."

"Does he have a motive?"

"If there is one, I can't see it. Belle Tackett practically raised him. I can't figure out what would cause him to make up a story about barbeque and movies. He's covering something up."

"So, young Mr. R.W. Seville is Suspect Number 1?"

"I'd say he's, at the very least, Liar Number 1. I have some ideas to follow and will get back to you. My second interview was with Buster McCombs."

I explained that Buster, whose full name was Jonathan Francis McCombs, had been feuding with the Tacketts for years. They live across the road from each other and there's a long history of bad blood, I told Phil. I also told him that Buster had not been honest about his activities yesterday, and I'd caught him holding back about his late evening whereabouts. That's why I still had some checking to do.

"Even though we all agree that he's a nasty piece of work, I'm not sure I see Buster as a killer."

Phil was only half listening because he had turned around to his computer. The screen offered up a three-course menu of information.

"What have we here?" Phil asked the computer.

He clicked on a few of the choices and grimaced. "Looks like your Mr. McCombs has quite a history. Arrests for DWI, assault and battery, resisting arrest, drunk and disorderly. Shall I go on?"

"I'm aware that he's had his troubles," I told Phil. "He's a Vietnam vet who drinks more than he should and has a chip on his shoulder. In spite of that, I don't see him as a cold-blooded killer."

"No one's a killer until they are," Phil said, pushing the print button to produce a hard copy of Buster's rap sheet. "I'm putting him down as our Suspect Number 2 with a big five-pointed star next to his name."

There was no reason to argue with Phil until I had more information. Best to move on.

"I had a long talk with the widower. Once Blake Tackett came out of his comatose state and began to answer a few questions, his story didn't hold up. No one can account for him at the Cattlemen's meeting after around three yesterday."

"What can you tell me about their marriage?"

"I've known both of them most of my life. They were married not long after high school. Blake was still at A&M when he proposed on the spur of the moment. It didn't fit what I knew about him. He's always been a planner. Some claimed Miss Lilly was what they call a 'honeymoon baby.'"

"A marriage of convenience rather than love?"

"Can't really say. They seemed to make it work."

"Any financial troubles or other problems that you know of?"

"The housekeeper, Hattie Mae Cooper, told me that she heard Blake tell his wife that he would be staying the night in Austin. I have reason to believe he came back to Lantz. When he stays in

Austin on Association business, he usually checks in at the Driskill downtown. It would help if your folks could check the hotel's registration records."

"Got it. So, the spouse is Suspect Number 3," Phil said, making a note. "In cases like this we usually look closely at the spouse. More often than not, we find what we're looking for. I'll put a star next to his name, too."

I began to get an uneasy feeling that Phil was jumping to conclusions, and I didn't like it one bit.

"Did you get anywhere with the daughter?" I could tell by his tone that he was still stinging a bit from his encounter with Lilly that morning.

"She's calmed down. Her boyfriend, Ed McCombs, gives her an alibi. They tell me that they spent the night together at the Driskill after the Cattlemen's meeting."

"So, we take her off the list of suspects?"

"Or add Ed."

Phil looked surprised.

I explained that Belle was hell-bent on keeping Ed and Lilly apart.

"Belle was obsessed and made life miserable for them both. I'm not sure that's a motive exactly, but after his time in the military, Ed has a hair trigger. For her part, Lilly has a lot of pent-up anger and a hot temper."

"I was on the receiving end of some of that this morning, you might recall," Phil said.

"They give each other an alibi. Right now, I'm inclined to believe them, but we need to be sure."

I asked Phil to add Lilly and Ed to the verifications that needed checking while his folks were talking to the Driskill management.

Phil jotted a note on his pad. "Who else?"

"I don't have much detail on Sara Evans because our interview was cut short. We grew up together and graduated high school in the same class. Me, Sara, Belle and the Three B's: Bobby, Blake, and Buster. Sara didn't make it past her first year in junior college. She took over at the Lantz General Store and a few years ago sold the double-wide she got in her divorce so she could move in with her ailing mother to take care of her.

"Why, exactly, is Sara Evans on the list?" Phil asked.

"For now, let's just say there is no love lost between her and Miss Belle, a story that goes back all the way to our high school days."

"So, Sara Evans is our Suspect Number 6."

"Until I can get more information about her comings and goings yesterday."

"That it?"

"One more."

Phil was too much of a pro to interrupt me when I told him the story of Belle and Ash Wednesday. If an expression came with subtitles his would have read, "You're shitting me."

"Do you think it was enough to give Bobby Seville a motive for murder?"

"I thought it was possible until you told me about the type of sedative in the orange juice and the fence wire around Miss Belle's neck. Bobby swears she was alive when he left. He tells me that he carried her upstairs and laid her across the bed and that was that. I still have questions. Something sloshing around in the back of my brain tells me there is more story there. When we found her, she was all decked out in her fancy bed clothes and the bottom of her booties were fresh clean. It was clear that she hadn't walked around after climbing under the covers. Undressing Belle and tucking her in that way doesn't sound like the Bobby I know."

"You say that he admits that they had it out."

I filled Phil in on Bobby's version of his run in with Miss Belle over Monica's ashes.

"He confronted her but he swears he didn't hurt her. I don't think he's lying exactly but I'm not sure we have the full picture yet."

"Let's call Robert Wayne "Bobby" Seville, Sr., our Suspect Number 7 for now."

"For now."

I flipped through my notes and scratched my head. Piss pot full of suspects and each and every one of them a friend. Made my head hurt and my stomach growl. I think Phil must have been reading my mind.

"I don't know about you but I'm ready for some home cooking," he said, pushing back his chair and grabbing his hat.

"Thought you'd never ask," I replied, packing up my paperwork. "Meet you there."

CHAPTER 13

One good thing about the DPS headquarters is its proximity to Threadgill's restaurant, known for dishing out home cooking and live music. Most folks from around here know the story of how Mr. Kenneth Threadgill helped launch the career of Janis Joplin when his place was little more than a converted Gulf filling station on what was then the far north end of Austin.

Fascination with the story of Miss Janis and Old Kenneth is easy to understand. It reads like a Greek tragedy. Small town girl with a heroic talent is befriended by a kindly wizard who lives in a shack on the edge of town. One day she's lured away by city lights and false promises. But there are demons in the shadows and her star burns bright until it flames out. It's been said that Janis had the Bells of Saint Mary in her chest. I figure that's about right.

I like to think it was Threadgill's woeful prayer when he ended his set each night that bound Miss Janis to him in the first place. That's when everybody would stop what they were doing to listen to him croon *It Is No Secret What God Can Do.* Women with hair-dos ratted high and wide would weep until eyeliner blacked their cheeks. Men whose hands understood the meaning of hard labor and coeds under the legal limit would close their eyes and hum along. Threadgill's crusty, melancholy anthem, full of forgiveness, gave them permission to lay down the anger, the mistakes, the lies, and the fuckups and start over. It was that side dish of redemption as much as the home cooking that attracted the hungry and the misfits.

Two FBI Special Agents who Phil knew from the local office were getting out of their car at the same time we were walking up to Threadgill's Back Porch entrance. They strolled over and said hello to Phil, and he introduced me.

"So, you're the legendary Sheriff Osborne of Arrowhead County," one of the agents said as he shook my hand.

"Wouldn't say that exactly," I replied.

"No sense being modest. Everyone in our office has heard about the mail tampering case you put together. Nice job, Sheriff," the taller one said, giving me one of his business cards. "Call me if you'd ever like to talk about a job with the feds."

I tucked the card for Special Agent Fuller Maxwell into my pocket without a second thought as they walked away. From the look on Phil's face, I could tell I wouldn't be able to eat in peace until I'd filled him in on the case. After we were seated in a comfortable booth away from the music, I gave him a quick answer to his inquiry.

"Just a greedy contract postal worker with sticky fingers. Believe me, Phil. It didn't take a genius to figure that one out. Let's order."

"I'll need more story," he laughed, studying the laminated fold-out menu.

I ordered the chicken fried chicken, which you might think is a bit of a redundant way to label something unless you are from Texas. Since it comes with two sides, I was all in for mashed potatoes and collard greens.

"Gravy on the side and greens in a bowl," I told the waitress, returning the menu.

Phil went in for chicken livers, black-eyed peas, and garlic cheese grits. He grabbed a warm cornbread muffin, split it in two and covered it with butter.

"Speak, my friend," he commanded, before filling his mouth.

This is the story I told him: I hadn't been Sheriff for long when our local radio preacher dropped by with some flyers he wanted to post at our window. His full name was Samuel Peter Thomas Burgess. Folks called him Rev. B.

Now this was a delicate matter, what with separation of church and state and all. When I explained the reason that I couldn't let him use our government bulletin boards, he shot right back with the fact that he didn't really have a church since he broadcast the good word. He said he got the inspiration for his radio show from the famous New York City evangelist Reverend Frederick J. Eikerenkoetter, known by everyone back in the day as Reverend Ike. He'd even adopted the Rev's catch phrase, "You can't lose with the stuff I use."

Rev. B, almost as wide as he was tall with an unnaturally curly crop of hair that he let grow past his ears, explained that he sold the promise of prosperity over the airwaves. Send in money for the ministry and you'd get a prayer cloth that Rev. B had personally blessed. Since no pulpit or sanctuary was involved, Rev. B figured he was good to go. It took me longer than it should have to get him to understand that "church" in the legal concept required for separation from government affairs had a broader meaning than a brick-and-mortar structure. It was rough rowing.

The time spent was worth it, however, since I learned a good bit about his operation during our talk. Seems he encouraged donations in cash to avoid the "devil's toolbox." By that I gathered he meant banks and their rules and recordkeeping and such that can be accessed by the Internal Revenue Service. He told his followers that the larger the cash donation, the more potent the prayer blessing he bestowed on the prayer cloth.

Now when I say cloth, it may take a little imagination to apply that noun to the items he mailed back to the true believers. His prayer cloths bore a strong resemblance to the spirit ribbons that we wore to high school football games with incantations on them such as "Bust the Bears" and "Flog the Frogs." Like our spirit ribbons in high school, his prayer cloths were no more than slim strips of acetate cut with pinking shears and imprinted with gold-flecked ink crosses. He explained that the power of the prayer was transmitted from his hands by placing the cloth in direct contact with whatever needed a blessing. A wallet for money. A pillow for a good night's sleep. A sore knee for pain relief. And on and on. Rev. B broadcast out of the back bedroom in his home so the mail came to his residential address.

Several months after my conversation with Rev. B, I was called to the scene of a highway accident. A pickup pulling a load of hogs had gone off the road and plowed into a dumpster behind a Valero filling station on the highway near Georgetown. No one was hurt in the wreck. However, a bunch of the hogs had escaped, causing all manner of chaos what with their rutting around in the bags of garbage that fell off the top of the dumpster on impact. Once we got the hogs and trucks sorted out, I stayed back to help the station owner sweep up.

That's when I saw the envelopes. Dozens and dozens of envelopes. All addressed to Rev. B's ministry. All empty. They were mixed in with junk mail and empty envelopes from paid bills. Thing was that the rest of the discarded mail was addressed to a different person. Curious, I gathered it all up and took it back to the station with me.

The addressee on the rest of the mail was none other than our friendly local postal worker, Jackson Pruitt. He wasn't an employee of the U.S. Postal Service *per se*. He was a contractor hired to deliver mail. I guess he liked the job because he was one of those whistle-while-you-work and tip-your-hat-to-the-ladies sort of fellas.

I thought about questioning Jackson, but something stuck in my craw. The dumpster was on the opposite side of the county from Rev. B's place. Didn't make any sense that some of his trash would wind up in a commercial dumpster twenty miles from his home.

Instead of questions, I decided to keep an eye on Jackson for a while. It didn't take long. Saturday was Jackson's last shift for the week. I followed him. Sure enough, he pulled over at one of those roadside rest stops that the Texas Department of Transportation built all over Texas some years back. They're outfitted with picnic tables and trash barrels. Ol' Jackson opened the hatch to his SUV and pulled out a zipper bag. I watched as he began to open the mail stashed in the zipper bag.

He was fast and efficient. This wasn't his first rodeo. When he was finished, he had a fistful of cash, which he transferred to a shoebox and then stowed it in the spare tire well of the SUV. He stuffed the envelopes into a trash bag and disposed of it in the roadside barrel. Fortunately for me, but not that much for him, I was recording on the dashboard camera of my patrol car. Got it all on tape. I took the bag of mail from the roadside rest stop and the videotape to the FBI. With my statement it was more than enough for a search warrant. They found more than $20,000 in shoeboxes. He'd apparently been skimming from Rev. B for months. He'd deliver about half the prayer requests and kept the rest for himself.

For some reason that he was never able to explain to anyone's satisfaction, Jackson had kept the notes and letters that were enclosed with all those small bills, mostly singles with a few fives and tens. They were a litany of human misery coupled with the eternal and undying belief in the power of grace:

> *"My little girl has terrible, rotten teeth and we can't afford a dentist. Pray for her to be healed."*
>
> *"I am a fornicator and I know it's wrong. Help me find forgiveness."*
>
> *"I have been buying a lottery ticket each week, but I never win. Please ask for Jesus to bless me with a winning ticket."*
>
> *"Daddy is still hitting Mama. Maybe you can send a stronger prayer cloth this time so that he will stop."*

"That's a hell of a story," Phil said as the waitress delivered platters of food and topped off our iced tea glasses.

We were hungry and the food was above par, so we ate without much more conversation before asking about dessert.

As much as I like to reminisce about the fine old days, the Threadgill's story that I'm most fond of has to do with angels—actually a movie about the Archangel Michael starring John Travolta. I wasn't all that fond of the movie itself. The thing it did have going for it was a scene that paid homage to pie, Threadgill's pie to be precise. Even on a bad day, you can't beat the pleasure of wrapping yourself around a slice of their strawberry-rhubarb. So, I did. Phil joined me. Then he asked for more story.

"What happened to Jackson?"

"He confessed. Got time in the federal lockup. The thing is Rev. B and Jackson have become friends. Rev. B visits him in jail on a regular basis and told me that he will give him a job once he's done his time. Rev. B says he does not think it is his place to judge or punish another human being. Then he quotes scripture at me, 'Vengeance is Mine; I will repay, saith the Lord.'"

"In other words, the preacher is living the Word?"

"That's one way to look at it."

"What's the other way?"

"What do you mean?"

"You said that was one way to look at it. What's the other way?"

"Well, I'd say it's every bit as likely that they're birds of a feather and Rev. B figured circumstances had blessed him with someone to help him carry out his mission."

"That's some next level redemption."

"Amen, brother."

"Amen."

CHAPTER 14

Phil promised to send me the results of tests on the fence wire they'd found around Miss Belle's neck as soon as they were available. He got a call before we left Threadgill's with verification from his officers on check-in and check-out times at the Driskill for everyone who said they were at the Cattlemen's Association meeting.

"Not bad for a day's work," I told him as he walked me to my car. He promised to call as soon as he had more information. Before he walked away, he asked me a question he'd asked before.

"Ray, when are you going chuck it in at Arrowhead County and come work with us?"

"When my Sweet Wife tells me I can," I said with a friendly slap on his back.

You might be surprised how often I get asked why I stay in a backwater like Arrowhead County instead of packing up and moving to Austin or some other big city. Phil always reminded me that the Texas Rangers had a need for what he called "talent" like me. I pretended to be flattered. I didn't kid myself. I figured it was code for easygoing folk who know how to fit in and not make waves.

Arrowhead County will always be a mystery to desk jockeys like Phil Ashworth. The county was carved out of a misbegotten piece of land when the surveyors were mapping Central Texas back in the early days of Texas statehood. Seems that the survey company that was hired to draw the maps was owned by two brothers who got into a nasty fight over a fair-haired woman. Their disagreement spilled into their job. The brothers split into two crews, turned separate work products into the state, collected their payments, and left. One brother went home to New York and the other set out for California. Their intent was to be as far from each other as their paychecks would allow.

Cartographers later discovered that there was a triangular-shaped piece of territory unaccounted for between Williamson and Travis Counties. Problems were easier to solve back in the day. Rather than send out a new survey crew to divide up the over-looked wedge between the two counties, they simply created another county. The shape inspired the name. Arrowhead is what you might call the Rhode Island of Texas counties. Loving County has fewer people, but Arrowhead has fewer acres.

Phil tends to think of Arrowhead and Lantz as quaint or, even worse, as cute. Problem is he doesn't appreciate the value of a quiet country road when you have a problem to solve. If you stand perfectly still on a Lantz back road you can feel the silence seep into you. I swear you can feel its breath on your neck as its arms wrap around your body and hold you close. When I get quiet like that I can sort through my problems and settle my mind to figure out what I need to do.

The first time I remember using the quiet to solve a problem was one summer after my sophomore year when I was fed up with college. My grades were in the toilet and my professors were giving me what for. I told my father that I was done with school. He didn't try to talk me out of it. He shipped me off to Midland to work in my uncle's roofing business. After eight weeks in hundred-plus temps hauling eighty-pound bundles of shingles around, I was on a late-night drive back to Lantz to have a heart-to-heart with my Pop. I was getting sleepy, so I pulled over onto the side of the road. The stars were tucked in behind the clouds and the moon was only a slit off on the horizon. The dark was broken by the distant flicker on the horizon that I figured was the light from a television visible through an open window of a house maybe a mile or two away. As I sat there and let the quiet do its thing, I was able to see how putting up with a little guff from tea-sipper profs in an airconditioned lecture hall wasn't such a bad deal after all. The anger and resentment I'd been feeling slipped out of me and I knew what I wanted to do. When I got home, I went straight to bed and slept for a day.

That's what I needed on the way back from Austin. I needed a quiet place to pull off the road and think. I'd collected a lot of information since I'd first stared down at Miss Belle's corpse. I needed some quiet to think about what I needed to do next. First, I had one more stop to make. Fortunately, there was enough light left in the day since my destination was just up the road from Threadgill's.

* * *

The six white stars that decorate the double metal gate of the Austin State Hospital Cemetery look nice from a distance. When you get up close, they suggest a poor man's Graceland entrance. I was lucky when I arrived because the gate was open. A work crew was repairing a damaged section of chain link fence.

The workmen waved as I pulled onto a white stone patch that passes for a parking spot. From the street it is almost impossible to tell that this state-operated burial ground is the final resting place for several thousand souls crammed onto a mere eleven acres, because only a handful of the graves have traditional tombstones. Once a quiet resting place on the outskirts of town, the cemetery now sits in the midst of heavily traveled commercial and residential streets where the city's nightlife encroaches ever closer.

Vandals periodically clip the fence wires on one corner of the graveyard to sneak in at night. This gives them access to the west facing wall of a bodega that abuts the field. They use the stucco as a canvas to paint flamboyant murals that are popular in this neighborhood. Right-wingers complain that it amounts to little more than graffiti. Liberals defend it as an expression of cultural street art. Regardless of the label, the result is a violation of the barrier that separates the sacred from the commercial and the broken fence inevitably must be repaired.

On the opposite corner, the one where I saw the crew working overtime, the fence faces a portion of the city street that makes a deep curve around the southwest corner of the graveyard. Motorists who ignore the speed limit frequently plow into the chain link, mowing it down.

Six or so scraggly hackberry trees, a handful of decrepit grave markers, and that pitiful fence are all that keeps what used to be called the Texas State Lunatic Asylum bound to this melancholy piece of its history. It doesn't look as if anyone spends any more time tending to the trees than they do the markers. Most of the graves are attested to only by flat pieces of numbered stone. The location of several hundred of the bodies don't even have that. Today's bureaucrats will tell you that marking the graves could run afoul of federal medical privacy laws. Perhaps. It's my humble opinion that it's more likely the distance families choose to put between themselves and what they consider a less-than-perfect relative. Abandoned in life. Forgotten in death.

That's what brought me.

Lucky for me, I remembered that Number 9H47F was three steps north of a grave with a distinctive tombstone. The Woodmen of the World marker is a four-foot-tall stone carved to resemble a tree stump and the only one like it in the cemetery. It makes Number 9H47F easy to find. I used my boot to scrape the overgrown grass from the marker and there it was. Number 9H47F. No name.

I remember my first visit as if it were yesterday. Buster, Bobby, and I drove Belle here after her sister passed. We were in high school. She'd found the letter from the Austin State Hospital asking her parents if they wanted to claim the body. They didn't. So, her baby sister, who'd been born four years after Belle, was buried without ceremony in what was little more than a pauper's grave. When we went to find Belle's sister all those years ago, we had to get permission from the groundskeeper who met us there to unlock the gate. It took some serious convincing. Even as a teenager, Belle could be persuasive when she set her mind to it. The stone was new then. No name. Only a number. Number 9H47F.

When she was a toddler, Belle treated Teresa Marie like a flesh-and-blood doll baby. She would rock her and play with her and sing to her. She couldn't understand why her parents took her away. They said Teresa Marie needed special care. The words they used didn't make sense to Belle who was little more than a baby herself. Teresa Marie wasn't expected to live long but she made it almost to her twelfth birthday before she passed. Belle was convinced that if Teresa Marie had stayed at home, she'd have been able to give her the care she needed. Belle never forgave her parents for sending Teresa Marie away.

Bobby and I slipped back to the car when Belle laid her bouquet of flowers on Teresa Marie's grave and started crying. Buster hung around a bit longer until he too drifted back to sit with us. Boys raised the way we were aren't good at tender moments. By the time Belle joined us she had traded her sadness for anger.

"Teresa Marie was mine and they took her away," Belle said. "They thought I'd forget but I'm not the forgetting kind."

By sending Teresa Marie away, Belle's parents were telling her that those who are inconvenient, those who are imperfect, are disposable. That is one of the ways that little girls get broken and a hard scar forms over the broken place. The cemetery was a sacred place to her. That's why when she asked me to take her back there, just the two of us, a few years later when she was hurting again, I did.

Looking down on that cold impersonal marker after Miss Belle died, I wished I had thought to bring flowers for Teresa Marie. All I could do was clean the stone a bit more with the heel of my boot and use my pocketknife to cut away some of the grass and weeds that were growing over it. Walking back to my car I couldn't help but wonder if Belle's way of hanging on to old hurts and striking out at those that crossed her had finally caught up with her.

One of the workers from the fence repair crew walked over as I was about to pull out of the gate. I stopped and rolled down my window.

"Here on business?" he asked, pointing at the Arrowhead County Sheriff's Office emblem painted on the side of my patrol car.

"Just paying respects," I answered.

"We're putting in a bit of overtime but gonna have to quit soon. Losing the light," he said, taking off his hat and gesturing toward the work underway on the chain link fence. "Old Bobby

Frost had it about right. Something in the world doesn't take to a wall."

"Or a fence neither."

"About right," he answered with a grin. "We put it up, but it'll always come back down."

"It's a job."

"About right."

CHAPTER 15

Can't think why I was surprised when Hattie told me that Miss Lilly and Blake Tackett along with Bobby and R.W. Seville were all at the Store drinking coffee as if it were any regular Tuesday morning in Lantz. It actually worked in my favor to have Hattie to myself because she had useful information that filled in missing pieces about Miss Belle's final hours. When I got to the Tackett place, she had Blake's sports jacket hanging up over the doorframe and was going after it with one of those lint rollers that work like inside out masking tape.

I'd wanted to talk to Hattie since yesterday morning, but it seemed like there was always something else that needed my attention first. While I drank coffee and Hattie worked on Blake's jacket, I asked her about the last time she'd seen Miss Belle alive.

"After I finished for the day, she asked me to set out plates and napkins. She was expecting someone. She didn't say who."

"I was under the impression that it was a regular movie night for R.W. and Miss Belle."

"Maybe, but I don't think so. She specifically asked me to put out the pink Depression glass luncheon plates. That is not a movie night choice of dinnerware."

"You seem mighty sure of that."

"Listen to me. I've cleaned house for that woman for thirty years, give or take. I know what she did to impress and I know what she looked like when she rolled down her stockings. That Depression glass was sending a message."

"What was the message?"

"You'll think I'm crazy."

"No ma'am. I will not."

"She bought that collectible glassware at a church garage sale after she heard Bobby's Monica admire it. If I had to guess, I would say that she was expecting Bobby for sandwiches."

I put my pen down and gave Hattie a look that I hope communicated, "and you're just now telling me this." It may have been lost on her since she chose that particular moment to leave the room with Blake's jacket.

"Be right back. Need to hang this."

When she returned, she dropped another bit of unexpected news on me.

"I guess you already know that Miss Sara came by after I left," she said, her back to me as she ran the sink full of water and began clearing the dishes. "I was up the road a piece when I looked in my rearview mirror and saw her turn into the Tackett driveway."

* * *

When I got to the Store, I could hear a loud conversation going on inside. It stopped mid-sentence as I opened the door and walked in. The first sound I heard was a voice over my shoulder.

"Well, now, if it isn't the man himself."

It was Sara, who'd walked in from the back room with a fresh pot of coffee and basket of hot biscuits.

"Good morning all," I greeted the folks at the table and then asked Sara for a cup of her coffee. "If it wouldn't be too much trouble."

I pulled up to the table and spoke to everyone without directing the question to anyone in particular. "How y'all doing? Holding up okay?"

Of course, it was Bobby who answered.

"How did things go down in Austin? Did you learn anything new about what happened to Miss Belle?"

"Actually, that's what I need to talk to Miss Lilly and Blake about."

Sara was hovering over my shoulder with that hot pot of coffee like she was trying to decide whether to pour me a cup or dump it on my head.

"Spit it out, Ray," she said. "You know we're all going to find out everything soon enough."

"That's up to Blake. He's entitled to the information first before everyone in town knows."

"Go ahead, Ray. We're family here," he said.

"It could be a game changer," I told him.

Before I could get in another word edgewise, Miss Lilly jumped all over me.

"What are you talking about? This is my mama. It's not a game."

"Poor choice of words," I replied. "Let me start over. As you all are aware, there was some kind of residue in the orange juice that Miss Belle drank. We all assumed it was connected to her death. Turns out that's not what killed her."

"I don't understand," Blake said.

"There is no easy way to say this," I said, hesitating and searching for words.

"Spit it out," Sara said.

"It's like this, Blake. The medical examiner found a wire around her neck. The stuff in the juice pitcher likely made her sleepy. She was strangled after she was unconscious."

"Oh my God," Lilly screamed, burying her face in her father's shoulder. Blake wrapped his arms around her in comfort and R.W. moved to her side, patting her shoulders awkwardly.

"Are you sure?" Blake asked.

"Pretty much. I'll know more once they've run a few tests. I feel you have the right to know," I answered.

"Where does that leave things?" Bobby asked.

"Damned if I know," I replied taking a drink of hot coffee that nearly scorched my tongue.

Sara slammed the coffeepot down and turned on her heel, making for the kitchen.

"We need to talk," I yelled to her retreating back.

"I've got cinnamon rolls about to burn in the oven," she replied without turning around.

R.W. handed Lilly his handkerchief and she wiped her eyes and blew her nose before addressing me. "If you don't know, Sheriff, who the hell does?"

"I'd say right now the only person who has a clear picture is the person that did this to your mama. I've learned a lot in the last twenty-four hours. The folks in Austin have made this case a priority. Give us some time. We'll figure it out."

I was hoping I sounded more confident than I felt.

"Ray's right, Miss Lilly," Bobby said, running a hand over his bald head as if to smooth down hair that hadn't been there for a long time. "You can't expect an overnight miracle. We've known Ray all our life. He's doing his best."

"His best may not be good enough," she said, standing up and pulling her keys from her pocket. "I need to go home now if that's okay with the Sheriff."

I signaled she could leave and she was out the door before anyone could say another word.

Everyone sat quiet for a bit before R.W. Seville spoke up.

"She's upset. Sheriff. This has been hard on her."

"I don't take offense," I told him.

Blake decided to follow his daughter as the next one to leave. "You need anything from me, Sheriff? I have work to do."

I was having a hard time getting used to the bitter tone Blake used when he said the word, "Sheriff," but swallowed that thought and simply answered that I'd come by later to discuss a few matters in private. He agreed. Bobby and R.W. Tackett polished off their coffee and followed their friend Blake out the door. I was contemplating a butter biscuit when I heard Sara behind me.

"You sure know how to clear a room."

"All part of my master plan to get you alone so we can talk," I told Sara in a way that I hoped she could tell I was joking. "We need to finish the conversation that was interrupted yesterday. Can you sit for a minute?"

I pulled out my notebook and flipped to an empty page, so she'd realize saying 'no' wasn't an option. "Tell me about the day Miss Belle died."

Sara sat down next to me and gave me a play-by-play. The day started like every other, helping her mother with breakfast and a bath before opening the Store for early arrivals.

"That included Lantz's favorite piece-of-work, Buster Mc-Combs?"

"It did. You know Buster. He always has a half-baked scheme to make money as long as it doesn't involve actually working."

"He said he'd been offered good money for a lease."

"I'll believe it when I see it."

She went on that it was a slow day because all the regulars were in Austin for the big Cattlemen's meeting. She said she was closing up early when Miss Belle called.

"Belle asked me to make up some sandwiches and drop them by her place. Ham and cheese and some of my homemade pimento cheese."

"With the crust cut off."

"Naturally," she said with a half-smile. "I bagged them up along with some chips and a pint of Blue Bell vanilla ice cream."

"Was anyone else at the Tackett place when you got there?"

"I didn't see anyone. Not even Hattie."

"What about Miss Belle?"

"Nope. Not even the Queen of Lantz her own self. When she called in the order, she told me to leave the food in the kitchen and put it on her charge card. I assumed she was upstairs because the kitchen door was unlocked. I yelled up the stairs to let her know I'd done as she asked and then I left."

"What time was that?"

"I had to drop Mama at her church. She was having a good day and wanted to spend time with some of her friends. I'm sure it wasn't much past two."

"Did you make sandwiches for Buster, too?"

"Excuse me?"

"He came to your house, didn't he?"

The door to the Store opened and four gray-haired women who looked like they were lost wandered in.

Sara jumped up to greet them.

"Welcome, ladies. How can I help you?"

"We'll have a look around, if that's okay," the lady in the front answered.

"Help yourself, and if you're hungry, we serve breakfast and lunch," Sara said, indicating the menu board hanging from the ceiling. She spit an answer into my ear before she started clearing away the cups on the table.

"Excuse me, but I have to earn a living."

"Don't we all."

"What does that mean?"

"We can't keep putting this off, Sara."

I could see that her customers needed her attention. I made an offer.

"After you close today? Where's good for you?"

She let out a slow sigh and told me she'd arrange for her mother's friend from church to stay late with her. Said she'd close around four o'clock and wait for me at the Store.

"Is that good enough for you, Sheriff?"

"Works for me," I said, finishing my coffee and tipping my hat to the customers as I exited. As luck would have it, I didn't make that appointment with Sara.

CHAPTER 16

I arrested Buster on my way back to the office. I clocked him going eight miles an hour snaking his way down a two-lane back road that had a little-to-nothing shoulder. The driver of a van with the distinctive Heart of Texas Pipeline Company logo on the side was laying into his horn and riding Buster's bumper. I didn't need a Breathalyzer to figure out that Buster was four-sheets-to-the-wind.

Buster passed out in my holding cell after I booked him and that's the way he stayed until he started thrashing and mumbling. Then he jumped up and yelled.

"Rats. Get the rats."

He was sweating and swatting at the air as he backed up against the wall of his cell. I'm not certain he was awake.

It didn't seem to faze Katie Brooks, who was working across from me at the office command center. She grabbed a squirt bottle of air freshener from the bottom drawer of her desk and hurried toward him.

"I'm coming, Mr. B. I'm coming."

She squatted down slightly pointing the trigger between the bars.

"Phew. Phew. Phew," she said, taking aim with both hands the way a kid might imitate the sound of a pistol, landing lavender-scented jet sprays onto corners of the bunk with practiced efficiency.

"Got ya!" she declared.

From where I sat there wasn't a rodent to be seen.

In a gentler tone, she addressed Buster. "You can lay back down now, Mr. B. They're gone. I got 'em all."

Buster returned to his cot, breaking wind in an impressive staccato as he curled around his pillow. Katie came back to her desk, pinching her nose.

"Bean burritos for breakfast."

"Does that happen often?"

"Beans. Greens. Milk. You name it."

"Not the farts. The screaming."

"Depends. Mostly when he gets liquored up. His head can get all twisted around like he's back in Vietnam. Mostly he goes on about his Army buddies, Sam Singer and Tater. Did he ever tell you that Singer had tattoos of naked women on his arms? He could make them dance when he flexed his muscles. Personally, I think tattoos are trashy. There are plenty of perfectly respectable girls these days who go to Austin to get pictures and such things drawn right onto their shoulders and arms and even their buttocks. I can't help but wonder how those tattoos will look when the girls get older and their skin wrinkles up. Do you think a tattoo of a flower will look wilted over time, or will it shrivel into a big ol' ink stain on their puckered-up skin?"

"We were talking about Buster and his rats."

"I do tend to lose focus," she giggled. "Daddy tells folks that I can start a conversation in Dallas, take a detour to Moscow, and wind up in Narnia. Have you ever read that story? Some say that the lion is a Christ figure. They argue about that in church sometimes because it is blasphemy to portray Jesus as a jungle creature. I worry about blasphemy because my daddy is one to take the Lord's name in vain whenever he drinks more than he should. I try to keep to the Commandments myself although I get confused sometimes about idolatry and such things. Do you ever get confused about idolatry, Sheriff?"

"Katie. What about Buster and the rats?"

"Right. Right. There I go dithering again. Sometimes Mr. B. calls 'em 'gooks.' Sometimes he calls 'em 'rats.' Mostly, it's bad dreaming and sleepwalking like today. Sometimes, though, the screaming wakes him up," she said. "I fetch him some coffee and leave it for him inside his cell. I don't want to embarrass him by asking too many questions. It's better if I turn up the radio to some good music and hum along while I work. If he wants to tell stories, I'm never too busy to take time to listen."

"What about the air freshener?"

Katie shrugged and grinned. "Daddy always taught me to keep an eye out for chances to kill two birds with one stone, as the saying goes. I don't personally think I could kill a bird. They are too pretty."

I must have looked annoyed because she backed off that side rail with a shrug and an "Oops."

"As you might have noticed, our Mr. B sometimes forgets to wash up. I figure it wouldn't hurt anything to inject a little freshness in his direction. When he's half asleep, he can't tell the difference between a squirt bottle and a firearm."

I hated to disturb Katie's concentration with more questions right then because I needed her to finish her budget magic for a meeting with the County Commissioners. As I already explained, Lantz isn't more than a bend in the road, but it has the dubious honor of being the county seat. The reasons are primarily geographic since Lantz is more or less in the middle of our triangular county. There are also political reasons I won't go into.

We don't have a courthouse exactly. It is an all-purpose government building made of Austin white limestone with a first-class red tile roof. The core of the building started out as a hacienda built by settlers on their Spanish land grant. It changed hands and purpose over the years until the county bought it. These days it rambles along on the edge of the parking lot in a lazy L-shape. Despite its architectural ambiguity, the building has survived tornados, fires, and all manner of political misadventure for more than a hundred years.

It serves as a one-stop municipal and government home to important things like the County Clerk and equipment for the Volunteer Fire Department. It is also the home for not-so-important things, such as space for the City Council and Arrowhead County Commissioners, the sort of folks that most of us would not miss one bit if they skipped a few meetings.

The features that I like most are the thick stone walls, which provide insulation from the God-awful Texas summer heat, the covered porch that runs the length of the front, and a tiled patio in the back that overlooks an open field with live oak trees offering plenty of afternoon shade. You can have your fancy courthouses in San Antonio and Dallas. The White House, which is what we call our all-purpose government building, suits me just fine.

My office, because of the one-cell lockup, has its own entrance. When I took over from the previous occupant, the place was a dump with broken furniture and obsolete technology. The desk chairs had been repaired with duct tape and the carpet smelled of mildew. It took some doing to clean things up and convince the powers that be to invest in a professional operation.

One thing I did keep from the previous administration was a hand-painted wooden sign on the wall that reads "Dura lex, sed lex." The former sheriff's daughter made it for him. I had to look it up. Latin for: "The law is harsh but it's the law." I figured that the old scallywag knew something I didn't. Besides, it covers up a hole in the sheetrock that to this day I still haven't gotten around to repairing.

Katie was working on my latest budget numbers to present to the County Commissioners for upgrades to our computer systems. The Commissioners didn't ask a lot of questions when I hired Katie to run the office. With the measly budget they'd approved, they must have figured I was lucky to get anyone to take the job. The high school principal had called to recommend her, explaining that Katie was a whiz at computers and accounting and had a near photographic memory for names and dates. The other kids in school mocked Katie for the way she dressed, her weight and her awkward, shuffling way of walking. High school isn't fun for a lot of folks. For Katie it was miserable. The principal almost begged me to give Katie an interview.

Katie's dad dropped her off a good half hour before her appointment since she'd never learned to drive. The mustard yellow dress with gigantic shocking pink flowers didn't exactly compliment her ample figure but you could tell by the way she held herself with pride that she'd spent time with her wardrobe selection that morning. Her handbag and sandals were also yellow, and she had butterfly barrettes in her hair that matched the flower garden bows that trimmed her dress. I would learn in the years that we worked together that matching was an essential element in her personal sense of style.

The budget session with the Commissioners was an annual song and dance. With Katie's numbers and groundwork, I always came out on top of any argument. She was about finished with the final printouts. I waited for her to wrap things up before getting back to the Buster story. I didn't have to wait long. She was ready to tell me more after she sent the report to the printer.

"Mr. B reminds me of my Great Aunt Willie. He tells stories, the way she did. I feel like he makes a lot of those stories up. I know for sure that she did. However, some of his stories seem like they come from a real place and time, just like the stories Aunt W. told me."

At the printer Katie began organizing printed sheets into sets for her report. "Her stories were about how things are and how they used to be, or at least how they should be."

She gave me the printouts and returned to her desk. "You know another thing? Mr. B lets me talk, too. Not everyone does that. It's nice."

"Now, Katie Sue, I don't believe I've ever heard anyone say something so kindly about Buster."

She reached into her bottom drawer for a Kleenex and used it to blow her nose.

"I guess I'm taken to mind about my Aunt W. I miss her something fierce. I remember the one time I visited her in East Texas. I got so excited about a downtown drinking fountain labeled 'Colored.' Before I could take a sip, she boxed my ears and yanked me away by my collar. I told her I only wanted to see what color the water was and if colored water had a different flavor."

Katie blew her nose again and reached for another tissue.

"When people nearby heard me say that they laughed and made fun. That really made Aunt W. angry. She yelled at the crowd and gave them the what for. Even when I messed up and did something stupid, she stood up for me." Katie blew her nose again.

"She tanned my hide when we got home," Katie said. "I don't know if she was put out at me about the water fountain or angry over the people who yelled at us."

Katie pointed out a few key numbers to make sure I was ready for the budget meeting and then her mind wandered back to her Aunt W.

"I loved my aunt until the day she passed on. Outside she was all anger and sharp tongue. People talked awful about her the way they do about Mr. B. Even though she acted like she didn't care, inside she was all torn up. When she was a little girl, something got broken and the pieces was put back together all wrong. Everything hurt after that, crooked and cracked and never quite right. That's why she didn't fit anymore," Katie said with a sniffle. "That's what I think, anyway."

"If you don't mind me asking, do you remember some of the stories Buster told you?"

The phone rang before she could answer my question and she reached to pick it up.

"Arrowhead County Sheriff. Katie Brooks speaking. How may I help you?"

She put her hand over mouthpiece. "It's for you, Sheriff. It's Miss Lilly and she is fit to be tied."

CHAPTER 17

Phil was reading Blake his rights when I arrived at the Tackett place. Lilly was on the phone with a high-priced Austin law firm. She hung up and went to her father's side.

"They'll meet you at the booking. You are to say nothing until then. Nothing at all. If they keep asking questions without your lawyer present, we'll sue them for violating your constitutional rights. Got that, Officer Ashworth?" she said with a bitter scowl at Phil.

She was just getting warmed up when she turned on me.

"Are you responsible for this, Ray?"

"Hold your horses. Let me talk to Phil."

I asked Phil for a minute in the kitchen. I wasn't exactly in a friendly mood.

"What the hell, man? Yesterday you were gathering evidence and running tests and today you swoop in with a warrant. What are you trying to pull here?"

"His fingerprints are all over the wire that was around his wife's neck. You said yourself his alibi is soft. We have him dead to rights."

"Where did you get his fingerprints for the match?"

"His prints are in our database because he has a license to carry a handgun. Perfect match with the prints on the murder weapon."

"Why didn't you call me?"

Phil didn't answer. He didn't have to.

"Let me see your paperwork," I demanded.

He handed over a warrant issued in Georgetown. Given the size and limited resources of Arrowhead County, our commissioners had entered into an Interjurisdictional Cooperation Agreement with Williamson County that Phil had used to get the warrant.

"Nice try," I told him, "But it requires the signature of an Arrowhead official."

"Got it," he said, flipping to page two.

County Judge Howard Puckett had signed off. I should have known it. You catch him before noon and he'd sign anything. I'd pulled that trick a few times myself.

"You got old Hangover Harold to sign off because you knew I wouldn't," I said without attempting to hide my contempt.

"It's a good case and you know it, Ray. We have the weapon. We have motive and we have opportunity."

"What motive?"

Before he could answer, Lilly was on top of us.

"Yeah, what motive?"

"We're not doing this here, Miss Tackett," he said, walking away.

Two officers walked Blake down the front stairs to the squad car with Lilly running after him screaming, "Don't say a word, Daddy. Not one word."

I was pretty sure she didn't have to remind him. He didn't look like he was in a talking frame of mind.

The drive to the Georgetown lockup was quick. Blake's Austin law firm sent a team lead by the name of Nancy Pearl Hawthorne. Even I'd heard of her. She cut her teeth on high profile criminal cases, including a couple of successful capital punishment appeals to the U.S. Supreme Court, no less. That is an impressive resume for anyone, especially in a state like Texas with a history not only of zealous incarceration but an affinity for the death penalty.

After Blake was booked and went through a series of interrogations by a highly frustrated Phil, Lawyer Hawthorne managed to get a quick arraignment for bail. Before the day was over Blake was on his way home. Even though his bank account took a hit, at least he would be sleeping in his own bed.

I caught up with him on the sidewalk outside the courthouse where Miss Lilly was waiting at the curb to drive him back to Lantz.

"Sorry about all of this, Blake. It's not the way I would have played it," I told him.

"Can't talk to you, Ray. My lawyer said I'm not to talk to the law unless she's present."

"I understand. Just wanted you to know that I'm not Phil. He pulled a fast one on me."

Blake climbed into the truck and slammed the door. I was still standing on the curb when Phil Ashworth walked up beside me.

"We need to talk about what happened in there," Phil said, gesturing toward the courthouse.

"I had to tell the judge the gospel truth. Blake is not a flight risk. Everyone who knows him knows he's never even left the state of Texas."

"You're too close to this, Ray. We have the goods. Everything points to him. If it walks like a duck and talks like a duck, then . . ."

I walked away for fear I might say something I would regret. Deep down I knew that Blake was no killer. But deep-down feelings didn't mean a rat's ass to cops once they get a suspect in mind. They start to build a case around that suspect and it's almost impossible to stop the forward momentum.

Phil is a good man and a good cop, but he'd made up his mind. He'd told the judge about some recent financial troubles that Blake had experienced and about a humongous life insurance policy on Miss Belle. He'd told the judge that no one could place Blake in Austin after three o'clock on the day of the murder and that Blake was being fuzzy as to his whereabouts. He'd told the judge that the fingerprints on the fence wire around Miss Belle's throat were a perfect match to Blake's fingerprints on file with the state. Three strikes. There was enough evidence to charge him.

My gut told me Phil had this one all wrong, ducks or no ducks. Trouble was I couldn't prove it. Not yet anyway.

CHAPTER 18

That evening I had one eye on the ballgame and one on Katie's budget spreadsheets. That's a lot of concentration after the kind of day I'd had, so when Buster sat up on the side of the cot, stumbled up behind me, grabbed the bars on the cell door and started talking, it rattled me so much I nearly messed my britches.

"Ray, there you are Ray. Good ol' Ray," he said. "I can trust you, can't I?"

He gestured with a desperate urgency for me to come closer.

"What do you need, buddy?" I asked, walking up to the cell, taking care to stay slightly off to the side to avoid the unpleasant smell, a blend of his funky breath and his piss-stained jeans. He'd failed to make it to the toilet at some point. A sound from the football game got his attention and he squinted at the television screen.

"Now that's something. Football. When we played in high school did you ever think it would come to this? You on that side of the bars and me on this side?"

"How about something to eat?"

I fetched a soda and some cheese crackers from the vending machine. I had to open the cellophane package and pop the top on soda can for him because his hands were shaking too bad to manage it. He sat down on the cot without taking a bite.

"I can't sleep with the noise them gooks are making banging and screaming on the inside of the can. Their rat ghosts are after me."

"What are you talking about?"

"You're a vet. You understand don't you, Ray?" he said, turning his back to me. "We only did what we were told." He cradled his head in his hands. "You can make them stop. You're the law. They have to stop if you tell them to. Tell them to stop."

I didn't say anything. I watched him rock back and forth. I was pretty sure I didn't want to hear the rest of the story, but it was clear that he was going to tell me anyway. It was festering and he needed to get it out.

"They were stealing from us. The lieutenant said to take care of it."

"Who was stealing?'

"The gooks. We caught 'em. Two little rat-hole shits."

"The VC?"

"It was Tater's idea. He said we needed to shove them in the trashcans and lock the lids. That way they couldn't run. I wanted to use an ice pick to poke air holes in the lid, but that Singer was a mean motherfucker. He's the one who collected trophies from dead soldiers. Sewed them on his uniform. The lieutenant never said nothing to him. The Louie was scared of Singer. Always made sure Singer was right next to him when things got rough. That's why he looked the other way when the bastard broke the rules."

"What did Singer do?"

"Singer said we needed to show the gooks who's the boss. Said we needed to take care of it once and for all."

Buster's hand was still so unsteady that when he tried to take a drink of the soda most of it dribbled out of the corner of his mouth and down his neck.

"It's not like we planned on eating 'em or anything like that. I swear to God, Ray, it wasn't me. It wasn't me who set the fire."

The shaking got worse and he started to curl up as if his middle was collapsing inward as the confession emptied out of him. He slouched over in a ball on the cot with his face to the wall. "You tell 'em to leave me be, Ray. They will listen to a lawman."

I knew that I wouldn't get anymore of the story. Besides, I'd heard all I could stand to hear. You don't need a play-by-play to understand what happened. The demon in Buster was exorcised, at least temporarily, and soon he was snoring. That's the problem with demons. When you let them out, they look for someone else to hook onto. Buster had let his out and now it had wormed its fangs into my brain.

"Thanks, Buster."

The trashcan story didn't come up between us again before Buster died. That didn't mean it ever stopped coming up in my feelings about Buster and how Vietnam broke him. Katie was right about one thing. When you get broken and the pieces get put back together wrong, you never heal. You never stop hurting. That was true for Buster and that was true for his nephew, Ed, too.

* * *

Ed McCombs once told me that there are some things you can only say to another veteran. It was one night when I was driving him home from The Rattlesnake Inn after he got into a bar fight with a couple of shavetails from Fort Hood. The three of them were sweaty and bloody when they staggered back in from the parking lot right after I arrived. The fight must have done them some good because they were slapping each other on the back and laughing about how the First Cav could kick the balls off the infantry on any given Sunday.

Tony, the owner of The Rattlesnake, said the fight started when the drunken soldiers made a nasty comment to Ed about cowboys taking their hats off inside. First thing you know the three were going at each other in the parking lot. Tony commandeered their car keys and called a friend at Hood. Then he called me. No one wanted the boys on the road until they'd slept it off.

The best route to Buster's place from Tony's was down a back-country road. There wasn't a moon that night and the stars were hiding behind clouds That's why I kept the car lights on bright and my eyes on the lookout for deer. Ed wasn't saying anything. I figured he'd dozed off. We were almost at the turnoff to his uncle's place when he startled me.

"Did things happen to you in the service? Things you don't want to talk about?" he asked.

"Not sure what you mean, son."

"There are things you can only tell another veteran," he said.

"Do you mean Afghanistan?"

"Uncle Buster tells stories from Vietnam. When he gets drunk." Ed's voice drifted and dimmed. Whatever he'd been thinking got sucked into the night. He didn't finish telling his story. Not that night anyway.

Before he had any more to say, I'd pulled up to the McCombs trailer. Some folks call it "manufactured housing." That's just slick sales talk if you ask me. Most of the corrugated metal siding was held in place with Popsicle sticks and bailing wire. The skirting had long since blown away, exposing a chipped and corroded cinder block foundation. All around it was tangled with generations of dead crab grass and dried choke weed. I had the distinct impression that the frame was bowed in the middle.

Tires and innertubes scattered on the roof didn't do anything to improve the looks of the place. Buster claimed he put them there to keep the roof from blowing off. Buster had also plastered the trailer with bumper stickers, most of which were sorely weathered with age. You could still read the one above the door, which read: "I wasn't here for the first American revolution, but by God I plan on being here for the next one." Kind of summed up Buster's brand of philosophical thinking.

Most of the yard, if you could call it that, was littered with rusted out farm equipment and a couple of cannibalized vehicles. They'd recently added a defunct yellow school bus from who knows where.

Ed didn't seem in a hurry to get out of my car.

"When you were in, did you deploy?" he asked me.

"I was strictly a weekend warrior. U.S. Army Reserve. One weekend a month in Austin at Camp Mabry. Summer training at Fort Hood."

I wasn't certain that he'd heard me because he sat for a while longer looking out the car window before he spoke again.

"It's not like you think it's going to be."

"What?"

"Killing."

Ed opened the car door and a couple of mangy cur hounds shot out from under the trailer barking and growling, ears laid back and teeth bared. He gave them an order, "Shut the fuck up!"

The dogs obeyed. Ed thanked me for the ride and wandered up to the trailer, the dogs, sniffing at his heels, almost causing him to trip over his own feet.

* * *

When Ed came to claim his uncle after Buster's night in my lockup, I thought back to that night I drove him home from The Rattlesnake Inn and what he said about killing. It may have meant nothing, but I had to consider it now that Miss Belle was gone. She stood in the way of his happiness and that, in any lawman's training manual, was a motive.

Ed brought his uncle a change of clothes and toiletries in a paper bag. Despite the constant aggravation he always came through for the old man. They both had the kind of war wounds you can't see. Since he'd been keeping company with Miss Lilly, Ed drank less and smiled a bit more. Maybe some of whatever happened to him over there was scabbing over. I prayed it was so.

Ed had Lilly.

Buster had Ed.

Buster was pretty near presentable by the time they were ready to leave.

"We need to talk later," I told them as they signed out. "A few questions about Miss Belle."

"Anytime," Ed said.

Buster gave me the one finger salute. He was back to his nasty old self.

Before he was out the door the phone rang. It was Sara.

"I waited over an hour for you, Sheriff. Did you change your mind about our meeting?"

"Sorry about that, Sara. I planned to call this morning and reschedule. Things went off the rails."

"I heard that a-hole friend of yours from the DPS pulled a fast one on Blake. What are you going to do about it?"

"I'm working on it. Right now, I need more information."

"We need to talk before things get out of hand."

"Agreed. Is now a good time?"

"I've got breakfast to serve and the Store to run."

"All I need is about half an hour for some basics. It will help Blake."

"Come now," she said and hung up.

I had good intentions, but circumstances were such that I stood her up again.

CHAPTER 19

Katie cupped her hand over the phone and gave me a look that was half excited and half puzzled.

"This caller says he's from the Federal Bureau of Investigation. We don't have a system set up for tracking federal cases, yet. Do you want to accept the call, Sheriff?"

"Did he give a name?"

"Says he's Special Agent Fuller Maxwell. Do you want me to get a badge number and check it out?"

"I'll take it."

She transferred the call and I picked up. It was one of the agents I'd run into at Threadgill's.

"Hi, Max. Did you like the pie?"

"This is an official call, Ray," he said in a tone that made me sit up straight and pick up a pencil. "Can you come to Austin or should I drive up your way?"

"What's this about?"

"I'd rather we do it in person."

"I kind of have my hands full right now."

I explained that I was in the middle of a murder investigation and that one of our most prominent citizens had just been booked by the DPS.

"This can't wait. It's confidential."

We arranged to meet at the Williamson County Courthouse in Georgetown's Downtown Historical District since it was halfway for both of us to drive. I told Katie to go find my sorry ass, part-time deputy to cover the office. Johnnie Lake is what they call a "must hire" in government parlance, him being the son-in-law of one of the County Commissioners and all. He's a good-looking boy and I suppose that he means well. I swear though that no one, not even Katie Sue Brooks, knows how he spends his days.

Once I located the conference room that Max had reserved at the courthouse in Georgetown, I saw that he was not alone. There were four other feds with him. He got down to brass tacks without introductions.

"Everything we say in here is in strictest confidence, Ray. Is that understood?"

"No problem. What gives?"

With a sweep of his hand encompassing the men and women around the table, Max said, "These folks are running an undercover investigation of a bribery scheme involving several elected officials, state and federal."

I must have whistled because a couple of them grinned.

"We have some wiretaps that picked up an unexpected exchange involving an individual you might recognize."

Now I was getting seriously curious.

Max told a technician at the end of the table to play the tape.

Two men who sounded like they were on speakerphone were talking about a piece of legislation that was about to come up for vote in Congress, something about feedlots and a bunch of mumbo jumbo that I couldn't follow. Cattle ranchers were all for the bill. On the other side, homeowners who lived near the feed-lots and some environmentalists were working to kill the bill. They argued it would pollute the soil, the water, and the air.

The way the ol 'boys on the phone saw it, the argument boiled down to whether you supported strong economic development or wanted to let things be run by a bunch of pussy tree huggers, or words to that effect. They were laughing and seemed to have had one too many bourbons when I heard a knock on the door.

"Howdy fellas."

It was a voice I knew all too well.

"I have those gratuity envelopes you asked for."

Sure as God made little green apples, it was the voice of the nicest man in all of Lantz, Texas, the tallest of the Three B's, my high school buddy, Bobby Seville.

Max motioned for the technician to stop the tape.

"Is that the only place you have him on tape?" I asked.

"Up till now. He wasn't the subject of the original warrant."

"I see."

"What do you want from me?"

"Tell us about Mr. Seville."

"Maybe you'd better be more specific. I've known Bobby most of my life. That means there's a piss pot full to tell."

A young woman dressed in all black with a high turtleneck and her hair pulled back in a ponytail interrupted. "Are you trying to be coy, Sheriff Osborne?"

"Sorry, I didn't get your name."

"I'm Special Agent Dupree assigned here from the Oklahoma Field Office to work on this Task Force. We've devoted months in time and thousands in taxpayer resources on this investigation. I'd say you need to quit stonewalling and show us a little of that famous Texas interagency coordination."

"Hold on, Charlotte," Max said. "Sheriff Osborne is a valuable resource. That's why I recommended we read him in on this."

"You said he was a sharp cookie," Agent Dupree responded. "I need to see some of that."

Her tone rubbed me the wrong way but I like to think it didn't show. What the hell does "sharp cookie" even mean? Why would anyone want to be, or even eat, a cookie with edges? Instead of saying what I was thinking, I slipped my best foot forward a tad.

"While I appreciate your confidence and all that, Max, I'm not sure what you want from me," I said. "You're the FBI. You can get all the information you need about Bobby. Hell, you probably already know more about him than I do. What can I add?"

"Good point," Max said. "We can subpoena all kinds of records. That's only paper. What we don't know is the man. That's where you come in."

I understood the unspoken question hanging over the room, and I didn't like the way it was making my stomach flip over.

CHAPTER 20

I'd decided to stop by the McCombs place on my way back from Georgetown. I'd already wasted a good part of the day dealing with the feds. My plan was to try to catch Buster sober and then to make peace with Sara since I'd left her hanging.

No one answered when I knocked on Buster's trailer door. I gave it a second try. This time I must have put a little more punch into it than I intended because the flimsy aluminum door swung open a crack. I pushed it open a little further to yell inside.

"Hey, Buster. It's me, Ray. Hey, Ed. Anybody home?"

Through the thin slice of open door, I could see enough to make out Buster's arm dangling off the couch. The dogs were sitting on the floor next to him, whimpering. Immediately, I thought, something's not right. From past experience, those two hounds would be charging at me instead of sulking. This was one of those cases we learned about in police academy of "reasonable belief of something not right." So, I pushed the door open and went in.

"Hey, Buster, what's happening here? You okay?"

The dogs looked up at me and then flopped their heads back onto their paws. The larger one made a half-hearted effort to use its tail to swat at some flies that were buzzing about. It didn't take a lot of police training to figure out why. Buster's head was lying on a pillow soaked in blood from the gunshot wound that had blown off most of right side of his face. A pistol was in his right hand. I felt for a pulse on his hand dangling off the couch even though it was clear from the wound that the man was gone.

I'm not embarrassed to say that it was a good thing the living room and kitchen consisted of one area because I had to empty my stomach and the sink was as far as I could make it. I splashed some water on my face and rinsed out my mouth before calling the office on my mobile phone.

"Katie, it's me."

"Hello, Sheriff Ray. What is your 10-20?"

"Katie, I don't have time for games right now. There's a situation here at the McCombs' place."

"What kind of situation?"

"A dead body situation."

"I do hope you mean a 10-45."

When I didn't give her the satisfaction of a response, she offered an interpretation.

"10-45. Animal carcass."

"No. I certainly do not mean an animal carcass and I told you to lay off all that talking in code." This time she knew I wasn't kidding. I explained what I'd found.

"You don't mean. We've got us two suspicious deaths in Lantz in the same week."

I gave her instructions to get word to Phil Ashworth.

"I guess that means we're working with him again."

"Until we have more information, I have no choice. We've got to assume a possible connection to the death of Miss Belle."

"Yes, sir. Anything else?"

"Do you have any idea where I can find Ed?"

"Not for one hundred percent sure, but rumor is he's been staying close to Miss Lilly since yesterday. They went to Georgetown to start making funeral arrangements. Blake said he'd leave the details up to her. Rumor is they didn't come home last night."

"Which funeral home?"

"I don't have that information right at this time. I can get it."

"You do that. And get Deputy Lake over here. I need him to help me secure this place until the Austin folks arrive. There are dogs. He'll need to bring a couple of crates."

"Where do you think Johnnie can pick up dog crates?"

"He'll have to use his imagination. Tell him to try the animal shelter in Florence and if that doesn't work tell him to try Georgetown. Get him moving. We need to do this fast."

"Over and out."

I hung up without answering Katie. I was in no mood. While talking to Katie I'd kept a close bead on the hounds. Even though the pups had stayed quiet, I couldn't count on that lasting and didn't want to rile them up. I decided to avoid any unnecessary movements until we had them kenneled. I took up a safe vantage point at the kitchen table and used the waiting time to make notes. I recorded my time of arrival and what I observed after I entered the trailer. I then snapped pictures of the living room and kitchen from where I sat.

It's odd how you see a place with different eyes at a time like that. I'd been to Buster's on-and-off over the years. Looking at it as a potential crime scene, I was taking in details as if I was seeing the place for the first time. The wall behind the couch was crowded with black and white photos in plastic Wal-Mart frames, most of them hanging all catawampus as if they'd been tacked up with no particular scheme or plan in mind. One here. One there. The longer I looked at them, the more I wanted to get up and straighten them. Like an itch you need to scratch. I used the camera zoom to take close-ups of each one, mostly to get my mind off how they tipped this way and that.

The place was not as dirty as I'd have expected given Buster's history. Now, that's not to say it was up to my mama's housekeeping standards. But the dishes were washed and stacked on a dishtowel next to the sink and the floor looked like someone had wet mopped it sometime in the last day or so. Knowing what I knew about Buster, I'd bet good money this was Ed's doing.

You wouldn't even want to consider taking such a bet after I tell you about the visit I'd made to the McCombs trailer the day before Ed moved back home. I was following up on a particularly serious complaint from the Tacketts about the sorry state of maintenance of the McCombs place. The Tacketts live across the road from the McCombs, and if ever there was a contrast in property maintenance it was the one between the McCombs and the Tackett spreads.

You might say the Tacketts were the kind of people who had exacting standards for everything from their toilet paper to their shoelaces. One look at their fence told the whole story. No post, no rail, no picket was out of plumb in that board fence enclosing Blake's 217 acres. Each footing was carefully set, exactly the same distance from the one before it. Like most things in Blake's life, his fence was executed with a precise plan in mind.

His outbuildings were fresh painted and he kept his equipment under roof so nothing would be exposed to the irascible Texas weather. Hell, at one point there was even a rumor going around that after it rained, Blake would wash and buff his cow's hooves to keep them from tracking mud. While I personally didn't put any stock in the notion of bovine pedicures, I do concede the point that Blake was persnickety. Even the trees that line the S-shaped driveway from the gate to his house were trimmed every year to perfectly frame his two-story Victorian.

Blake's reward was an unobstructed view across the road where the McCombs' homestead offered God's very depiction of decrepitude, ruin, and disrepair. One look at the McCombs fence was all you needed to understand the problem. It was an embarrassment of three rusted-out barbed wires strung haphazardly along posts cut from misshapen tree branches that look positively arthritic. I can't tell you why Buster bothered with a fence at all since he didn't keep stock. He used to have a few jennies and a couple of donkeys, but they long since disappeared. Junk was the only thing he was fencing in. Tons of junk. I swear there were times I wondered if Buster invited folks to use his yard as a dump to irritate the Tacketts.

Buster swore he didn't have the first idea how the heap of tires, derelict appliances, discarded furniture, mopheads, broom handles, broken toys, rusty bits of who-knows-what got there. Once when he was lit up, he told me that he woke up in the night to some suspicious moaning coming from one particularly insidious mound. The next morning, he swore that the subject pile had doubled in size. He licked his lips and looked at me as if he was about to tell an off-color joke.

"It's like this, Ray. I believe that I'm the victim of what you might call, for lack of a better term, 'trash heap procreation.' Get it?"

His alcohol-numbed mind thought he'd made a first-class joke, and he was expecting me to laugh. That's how far he'd slipped by then.

The Tacketts had complained before, yet on this occasion, they had their Austin lawyer contact me. He was loaded for bear, citing precise fencing standards set out in Section 143.028 of the Texas Ag Code as well as regulations from the Texas Commission on Environmental Quality. For good measure he threw in a few citations from the Texas Health & Safety Code. He went on with a recitation and citations for such a long time that once I'd filled up three pages on my yellow legal tablet, I stopped taking notes and listened. What worried me most were some serious fines for improper disposal of abandoned tires, which are considered both an environmental and health hazard. I remember him specifically mentioning that abandoned tires can become mosquito incubators after a rainstorm.

You might say he was ready to kick ass and take names. He said the Tacketts were willing to let the county sheriff, yours truly, see that Mr. McCombs came into compliance. Otherwise, they had authorized their legal team to move forward with the appropriate government agencies. I took note of the way he said, "come into compliance." Lawyer code for, "I mean business."

Complaints from the Tacketts were so common that I was afraid Buster might not take my call seriously. That's why I went to see him in person. I got there late in the afternoon. His spindly front door was hanging open. When I say hanging, I mean that literally. Only one screw held the door on the hinge. Inside, Buster was plastered, and I got a good dose of what the lawyer meant by mosquito incubator. The place was swarming. Buster was passed out.

The layers of putrid smells signaled that the plumbing was backed up and since my shoes stuck to the floor as I walked through the door, I figured no one had bothered to do any cleaning for quite some time. I leaned over to shake Buster's shoulder without noticing the pistol lying next to him.

"Hey, Buster, wake up." Before I could say another word, I had a Browning High Power 9mm in my face.

"Touch me again and I'll blow a hole through your ugly face," Buster growled, his eyes half closed and out of focus.

Now, Buster and I go way back, and I'll give him a lot of leeway for what he's been though. But not that. I knocked the gun out of his hand and planted my knee in his chest. He passed out before I could cuff him. I called Johnnie Lake to come help me.

By the time we'd hosed Buster off and found a set of almost-clean clothes for him to change into, he was conscious again and acting a bit more like his ordinary, ornery self. That isn't necessarily a good thing. He projected a case of amnesia and asked why he was under arrest. I didn't want to spend any more time than necessary in that nasty trailer. We loaded him up in the patrol car and headed for the station. I'd called ahead for Katie to start brewing strong coffee and to order some burgers from the Joe's Place. Buster didn't look like he'd eaten in a while.

Buster had a mouth full of Joe's waffle fries when his nephew, Ed, showed up. Ed had just mustered out of the service. Although he was in civvies, his hair was still cut high and tight. Ed greeted Katie with open arms as she ran to hug him. Then he spotted his uncle and all the joy melted from his face.

"What's he done now?"

CHAPTER 21

Once Ed had moved in with Buster he started "shoveling shit," as he so colorfully labeled the clean-up project that seemed to be without end. He took on two jobs. The place needed more repairs than one man could handle in his non-existent spare time, but the size of the junkyard dwindled, and before long he had the plumbing and septic system functioning. The ball-busting Austin lawyer backed off because he could see that Ed was making a good-faith effort to clear away the worst of the accumulated trash heap.

Inside the trailer presented a different kind of challenge, yet soon it, too, began to yield to Ed's elbow grease. The smell was now less like a public toilet and more like a basement that needed to be aired out. My nose told me there still must be mold somewhere from years of deferred maintenance, but I could tell Ed's hard work had paid off. Until today.

The dogs didn't seem to be stirred up as long as I was willing to minimize my movement. I spent the time thumbing through the digital file of the photos I'd taken. They pretty much touched on all the milestones of Buster's life. There was one of him as a kid with his Mom and Pop and older brother, all long since gone.

There was one of the four of us in our high school football uniforms: me and the three B's—Blake, Bobby, and Buster. Jesus, how could anyone look so young and stupid? Buster had even framed his high school cap-and-gown graduation picture. Didn't know he was sentimental.

There were several from his Army days. One was of him in Vietnam standing next to six buddies holding a Texas Lone Star flag. I'd forgotten about that one. Good-hearted Bobby Seville had pulled some strings with a friend of his father to snag a flag that had flown over the Texas Capitol and sent it to Buster's unit. There was a system at the Capitol where a crew climbed up to the dome one day a week and ran flags up and down the pole for a few seconds at a time. The souvenir came with a certificate giving the date it flew over the Capitol. From the shit-eating grin on his face, you'd think Buster had just won the lottery. I zoomed in on the faces of the other GIs holding the flag and wondered if any of them were his friends, Sam Singer and Tater, from that awful trashcan business.

Looking at those photos, you had to wonder how the handsome boy in the Lantz football uniform became the Buster lying over there on the couch with his head half blown to smithereens.

Every framed photo on the wall was black-and-white save one. It was a color picture of Diamondhead in Hawaii. I was pretty sure it was a framed postcard. I made a mental note to take it out to see if there was anything written on the back.

* * *

My phone rang, which set the dogs to growling. It was Phil Ashworth.

"Did you get my message?" I whispered.

"Speak up."

"Can't. Got some angry canines here."

"Canines? What are you talking about?"

I covered the phone with my hand and spoke softly.

"I'm in confined quarters with two nasty excuses for dogs who would as soon tear me a new one as look at me. I'm trying to keep the lid on until I get backup."

After a bit more of the back and forth, Phil explained he was sending a crime scene investigation team. He couldn't join them right away.

"They're top-notch people and will do a good job," he assured me.

I will admit I had mixed feelings. After our sharp words following Blake's arrest, I wasn't sure where I stood with Phil. I trusted him more than most of the Austin folks. At this point, though, that wasn't saying a lot.

Before I could sort out how I felt, I had to sign off because Deputy Lake showed up with animal control specialists. I confess my blood pressure likely dropped several notches after they crated the critters and left.

Miss Lilly and Ed arrived not long after Phil's team of investigators started working the scene and began collecting evidence, taking photos, and preparing Buster's body for transport. Lilly stayed right by Ed's side the whole time they questioned him. Lilly and Ed stood with me in the kitchen area while we watched the team finish up.

"Well, Ray, at least this is one they won't try to pin on my daddy," Miss Lilly said, her words bitter. "He was in custody when Buster died."

I decided it was best not to answer. Besides, we needed to get out of the way. It was time for the team to move Buster's body.

Ed walked with Lilly hand-in-hand into the yard, where all three of us watched in silence as they loaded his uncle's body into a van and slowly pulled down the gravel road and across the cattle guard to the highway. With a great big hole in Buster's face, an autopsy seemed unnecessary to establish the cause of death, but it might produce other useful information.

Ed didn't seem to mind the delay given the sorry state of his uncle's affairs. He would need a little time to make plans. Lucky for him, he'd insisted his uncle sign a Power of Attorney when he moved in with Buster so he could hire day laborers, buy supplies, and get the lawyers off their back. It gave him broad legal authority to act on Buster's behalf. It would come in handy now.

Once the trailer was cleared of official folk, we went in and looked around. There was no way Ed was going to be able to spend the night there. The couch was covered in blood and the forensic team had made a mess of everything else, not to mention what was left behind by a pair of nervous dogs who hadn't been walked in hours. I called Phil for confirmation that the forensic folks had all they needed. He gave the go ahead to clean the place.

Lilly took charge. She called Hattie and asked her if she would call some folks and assemble a cleaning team to mop up the place and haul the couch to the dump.

"Take anything else that's got the death stink on it, too," Lilly told Hattie, giving Ed a look that was only partly a question. His response was no more than a blink of both eyes and a slight tilt of his head. Lilly took it as agreement. Naturally, Hattie didn't hesitate, promising to be there as soon as she could round up a crew.

Got to love Hattie.

Lilly asked Ed if he needed an overnight bag because she wanted to go back to Georgetown.

"We'll stop by the house to check on Daddy first."

"I don't think he'll like it," Ed said.

"You leave him to me. I know how to talk to him," Lilly assured him. "He needs some time alone to sort out all the business with the police and Mama and all."

"Where will you be staying and when will you be back?" I asked.

"What's it to you, Sheriff?" Lilly snapped.

"I have questions for both of you," I said without flinching. "I'm happy to give you two time to collect yourself even though you understand this is a police matter, and I can't let it ride. You do know that don't you, Ed?"

"You're right, Ray. We appreciate the way you've handled things. How about tomorrow morning?" Ed said.

"Let's meet back here at ten," I said. "Should give Hattie enough time. I'll lock up."

Lilly indicated agreement and then outlined her plan for the evening.

"I'll book Ed and me overnight at a B&B. I've stayed there before. The Harty House is a couple of blocks off Georgetown square. The last thing either of us needs right now is the kind chaos that goes on in a hotel," Lilly said, tucking her arm into his and leading Ed out the broken trailer door.

I watched them drive away in Lilly's truck and wondered if I'd screwed up, letting them leave the "crime scene" before interrogating them. Looking back, I think I was motivated in equal parts by my need to spend what energy I had left in my bones to get ready for a six o'clock Commissioner's budget meeting and by a growing conviction that after what he'd pulled with Blake, I didn't give a rat's ass what Phil Ashworth or anyone else at the DPS thought of my policing decisions.

Six o'clock was just an hour away and I needed to swing by the house for a quick bite to eat and a little time to decompress with S.W. Even though Katie Sue had the budget numbers ready to go, it was always a fight with the knuckleheads on the Commissioner's Court to make them understand the basic needs of running a modern sheriff's office. If they balked, I would once again have to remind them how I came to the job. It did the trick every time.

I'd been elected Sheriff of Arrowhead County when we lost our dear departed sheriff to a heart attack in what you might call a compromising position, that position being the four-poster bed of a female who was not the one he was married to. When the Commissioner's Court called an audit, they found he'd violated more than his marriage vows. His travel vouchers were as crooked as a three-dollar bill and no one could make hide nor hair of his arrest records and accounts since the little lady he was sleeping with hadn't bothered to show up at the workplace for months.

Long story short, they called a special election and appointed me as temporary sheriff because I'd had Military Police training in the Army Reserves. Since almost nobody votes in a special election, I won hands down. If I had it to do over again, I'm not sure I'd take the job. I was still cleaning up the mess left by the previous administration. They couldn't afford to have a repeat of what happened in the past.

With Katie's help, or should I say with Katie's ingenuity, we are on our way to a modern computer data system and record keeping. I had to hold their feet to the fire to keep them from reneging on their promises.

Like the sign says: Dura lex, sed lex.

CHAPTER 22

The next morning we were back at Buster's place pulling his old military footlocker out from under his bed. Hattie's crew had the place smelling clean with all signs of yesterday's tragedy scrubbed away. Bobby Seville got there not long after Miss Lilly and Ed. He told us he'd been at the General Store when he heard what happened to Buster and came straight away to see what he could do to help.

I'd have bet you my daddy's gold tooth I knew about all there was worth knowing about Buster McCombs before Ed opened his old Army trunk. I'd have lost that bet.

Even though the olive-green paint was faded and peeling I could still make out Buster's name, rank, and serial number stenciled in block letters on the top and side of the footlocker. Ed sat cross-legged on the floor and took a deep breath before popping the metal hatch.

The three of us, Bobby, Miss Lilly, and myself, watched while Ed lifted the lid. The top tray had bundles of yellowed letters and greeting cards. Most were held together with rubber bands, which had turned to a sticky green goo with age. Ed unpacked the tray, stacking the bundles on the bed.

Lilly sat down on the bed next to the stacks. When she picked up a bundle the rubber band gave way and the letters scattered across the bed. She took a letter from its envelope. A puzzled look settled on her face after she'd read a few lines.

"Listen to this. It's from Mama."

Hello Soldier Boy,

I am soooo excited to actually know someone personally who is actually fighting in a real war zone. The girls in the dorm ask me all sorts of questions about you. You are as brave as you are handsome. I watch all the news about Viet Nam on television hoping I will see you. I can only imagine how it must feel to be right there in the middle of things, fighting for our country.

You aren't missing anything here. If you think Lantz is dull as dishwater you should see Commerce. There're more students on the ETSU campus than in the town. I go home most weekends to get my laundry done and catch up on local gossip. Ha. Ha.

Bobby S. and Blake T. are setting the world on fire at A&M. Most popular this. Most popular that. By the way, have you ever heard of the "12th Man"? Well, your old high school buddies are totally into it, standing for the whole football game to show support for the team on the field. If you ask me, it is stupid. There you are fighting for our country and they are acting like children, getting all hyped up over football. Really? Grow up! I think you are much, much more mature and brave. I believe in my heart you will come home a hero.

Your friend from the "home front,"
Belle

Lilly riffled through the envelopes, opening several, looking at the handwriting and addresses.

"I think they're all from Mama."

"Who are they addressed to?" Bobby asked.

"Who do you think?" Lilly replied.

"Not Buster," he answered.

"Of course Buster," she said.

"When were they written?" Ed asked.

She looked at the postmark on several. Then picked up another stack and then another. "From the addresses and dates, I'd say while he was in the service."

"Dadgum." Bobby said. "Do you think your daddy knew?"

She gave him a who-the-fuck-knows look. Ed had stopped listening and lifted the now empty tray out of the footlocker. Folded neatly below was Buster's army uniform and a regulation dress shirt.

"This is what I was looking for," Ed said, standing and giving the dress greens a good shake. I'll take this all to the cleaners."

Underneath the uniform were a forlorn Garrison cap, a pair of black dress shoes in need of a good spit polish, and a paper sack. Bobby emptied the sack. Inside were Buster's nametag, discolored with age, his army service insignia, a couple of military ribbons, dog tags, and a belt with a tarnished buckle.

"This'll shine up right fine with a little Brasso and elbow grease," Bobby said, spitting on the buckle and rubbing it against his jeans.

"You planning on an open casket?" I asked.

"Nah. Wouldn't work, you know," Ed said with a sigh. "He'd want to be buried in his uniform, regardless. I'm going to talk to the funeral home in Killeen since those folks know how to deal with veterans and military affairs what with Fort Hood close by. They'll get him looking sharp and squared away. They'll also be able to help me work with the Veteran's Administration regarding burial benefits."

Lilly was riffling through the letters on the bed when Ed found an envelope in the inside pocket of his uncle's uniform jacket.

He pulled out a faded, but still legible, copy of Buster's DD-214. He unfolded it carefully to make sure the fragile paper didn't rip.

"Way to go Uncle Buster," he said. "I'll need this."

A second piece of paper was a one-page, handwritten document. He skimmed it and folded it back up.

"Buster's will," he explained.

He felt a bulge in the envelope and dumped it into his hand. It looked like a safe deposit box key. Ed gave the will and key to Lilly.

"Will you hold these for me?" he asked her. "The funeral home will want a copy of the DD-214 since it's the official record of Buster's military service."

"Can I take a quick look?" I asked.

"Sure," Ed said and passed the government document over to me.

I gave it a cursory review and returned it to him. "I'll need a copy. If you don't mind. I'd like a copy of his will, too. For my file."

"Okay if I bring those by later?"

"Sure. Can I ask about the key?"

"He banked over in Killeen. I have access to his account. This is the first I've heard about a box. One more thing to figure out."

"When you find out, I'd like to be there when you open it. If we need to make an official request for access, I can help."

"Sure, no problem."

The folks in Austin would probably pitch a conniption fit if they found out I let the paperwork and key out of my possession. At that particular moment, I didn't give a rat's ass what they thought. I knew that I'd do a whole sight better by earning Ed's trust than by throwing my weight around.

Ed set the tray back in the footlocker and reached for the letters. It was clear to me Lilly didn't want to let them out of her hands, and I definitely wanted to get a better good look at them.

"Bobby," I suggested, "Why don't you drive Ed over to the funeral home and help him talk to those folks. I'll stay with Lilly and we'll clear things up. I imagine Miss Lilly has had her fill of funeral homes for now."

"We'll take mine," Bobby said, jingling the keys to his Ford pickup.

"Okay with you, Lilly?" Ed asked.

"I'll be fine," she said.

"Do you mind if I take a look at what's in Buster's trunk while I'm here?" I asked Ed.

"Have at it," Ed said, with a sweep of his hand as he left.

I waited until we heard Bobby's truck pull away before I said anything to Lilly.

"Are you sure you want to do this?"

Her answer was to pick up another letter and open it.

Dear Buster,

Oh, My Mercy! I nearly fainted when I opened the package. A real string of pearls from the Orient!!!! The girls in the dorm are freaking out. You are too, too sweet to me. I put it on the minute I opened the box and haven't taken it off. Too bad I will have to hide it when I go home. Mama is such a snoop. She would not think it proper for a girl to accept such an expensive present from a boy. She is soooo old fashioned.

Tonight, there's a football game and I promised to go with some friends. We're going for pizza after. There is NOTHING to do in this town. This place is soooo lame.

Yours in gratefulness, Belle

P.S. I hope you don't mind but I told the girls the pearls were from my "boyfriend."

"Did you know about any of this?" I asked her, pointing to the letters in her hand.

"I've suspected Mama wasn't exactly a virgin when she married Daddy. But Buster? Not in a million years."

"Your problem is you didn't know him as a young man. The war changed him," I said. "Hell, it changed us all."

"Thing is, Mama talked about Buster like he was an uncouth dog. It was Mama who was behind all the official complaints about this place. Daddy was willing to let things slide. It was Mama who hired the Austin law firm to go after Buster before Ed moved in. Why would she say all those awful things if they were once. . .? I don't know. Whatever they were."

"Do you know anything about the pearls?"

"Not a necklace but there are those big pearl and diamond rings. Maybe she had them made up from the necklace pearls. She never said," Lilly sighed. "Apparently, there's a lot she never talked about."

"You may not like what we find here."

"I already don't like it. Let's get started," she said, reaching for another letter.

CHAPTER 23

Lilly and I sorted the letters into three stacks. The first group was addressed to Buster at Fort Polk, where he was sent after he enlisted. It didn't take long for basic training to knock a lot of the red-white-and-blue right out of Buster. The climate in that part of Louisiana mirrored the kind of heat and humidity in the Vietnam wetlands, which made it ideal for training soldiers before they were shipped to country. Buster once told me that the enlisted men at Fort Polk had a saying: If God wanted to give the world an enema, Fort Polk is where he'd stick the hose.

At first Buster seemed to lean into the military life where everything was prescribed and orderly with neat rows and numbered buildings, dress codes, no ambiguity, no room for invention or nuance. Eventually, the sameness must have worn on him. Buster's loss of patriotic fire was all there in Belle's letters. Her earliest letters were full of local gossip. Later she seemed to be responding to a boy whose spirits were fading. They were as much notes as they were letters, full of the kinds of saccharine encouragement you'd expect from an eighteen-year-old girl. She told him to "hang in there" and "don't lose your way."

"No disrespect but some of this is dull as dishwater," I said after reading a handful.

"None taken," Lilly said with a chuckle, handing me another of batch of Belle's attempts to boost Buster's morale. "Do you think she copied some of this stuff right out of greeting cards at the drug store?"

You had to hand it to Belle, what she lacked in originality she made up for in persistence. She kept up regular correspondence for months, like a lifeline you want to assume was at least in part a response to a call for help from Buster. Sometimes there must have been actual phone calls because Belle would mention how much she enjoyed their chat and was looking forward to another.

Belle wrote the second batch of letters to Buster while he was stationed in Vietnam. They were easy to identify because of the paper-thin envelopes trimmed with the red hash marks that were required back in the day to signal airmail to an APO or Army Post Office address. We read them in sequence skimming most of them since they were often college girl gossip and repetitive, offering little in new information.

Then we got to one about Sara.

Hello Buster,

It is crazy hot and dry here in Texas. I saw a report on the news you are getting a lot of rain over there in Viet Nam. Please send some our way. Ha. Ha.

You'll never believe who I saw out with Blake T. It's that cracker Sara Lawrence. Everyone knows she was born on the wrong side of the blanket. She never even finished junior college. Did she? Mama says she is trailer trash. That's why she made sure I didn't associate with her in school. Now she's mopping floors and waiting tables at the General Store. Where does she get off thinking she's good enough for Blake? Everyone knows

Blake's daddy is as rich as chocolate cake. Well, I never!! (Do you think maybe she and Blake are sleeping together? Never mind. That wasn't a proper question. Ha. Ha.)

I have big news! I'm going to quit college. The counselors here at ETSU think I should change my major to elementary education. Can you believe it? I can't imagine myself in a classroom teaching someone else's snot-nose kids. They think my grades in core classes don't hold up for a major in another field. What do they know? I'm not coming back next semester. My parents are going to be sooooo mad at me. Pray I don't get horse whipped. Ha. Ha.

Stay sweet,
Belle

Miss Lilly handed it to me with a sour expression on her face. "You know, Mama was wrong-headed about Sara. I could always tell Sara things I could never tell my own mother."

"What kind of things?"

Lilly cocked one eyebrow at me as if I had asked a question I had no business asking and clammed up. I could feel the energy between us change.

"Tell you what. Let's take a break," I suggested. I stood and stretched, but Lilly stayed where she was, cross-legged on the bed surrounded by the letters.

"I'll see what's in the fridge," I offered, excusing myself.

It was mighty slim pickings. The McCombs boys apparently didn't go for a lot of home cooking.

"Hey, Miss Lilly," I called in to her. "We've got a box of Drum-stick ice cream bars in the freezer and a package of Flamin' Hot beef jerky. Take your pick."

"I'll pass," she yelled back.

Had to agree with her choice. When I returned the jerky to the plastic shopping bag where I'd found it, I noticed a receipt in the bottom of the bag from the Chevron station across the street from the Veterans Memorial on the main highway through Florence. The Memorial would be easy to miss driving through town because it's set off to the side and not much tells you it's there. If you pulled off the main street and took a look, you'd see the names of local vets who died in every war since the Civil War inscribed on the sides of the slabs of granite encircling a flagpole. The monument meant a lot to Buster and his VFW buddies, and they made a point of stopping by on a regular basis to clean up the trash, wipe bird droppings and dust off the stones.

Since the receipt timestamped the date and time of the purchase of gas and the jerky and Drumsticks, I pocketed it. I spotted a couple of sodas shoved in the back of the bottom shelf of the fridge and brought them to the bedroom to share with Lilly.

"Look what I found," I showed Lilly.

We each popped the tab and drank straight from the can. Funny how sharing a little refreshment can improve the mood.

"You were talking about your mama," I said, leaving the subject open ended.

"Mama was never satisfied. Enough was never enough. If you made the team, why weren't you elected captain? If you won the game, why didn't you win district championship? If you won district, why didn't you make state? She was always upping the ante on you. Sara's philosophy is different. If something went wrong, she'd remind you it's not that you've lost, it's that you haven't won yet."

We sat for a bit sipping soda and not saying anything. I thought that was all Miss Lilly was going to share. Turned out she was just getting wound up.

"I know this much. The girl who wrote these letters is not the woman who raised me."

Lilly finished off her cola and looked around for a place to get rid of the can. I took it from her and polished off mine, taking the cans to the kitchen to toss.

Returning from the kitchen she told me, "I know you've been trying to talk to Sara about Mama's murder. You're on the wrong path there."

"I'm listening."

"When I moved back to Lantz from Austin, I gave up trying to be the daughter Mama wanted me to be and decided to be the woman I wanted to be. It was Sara who helped me figure stuff out."

I sat back down in the chair next to the bed and waited.

"It's a long story," she said.

"Like I said, I'm listening."

CHAPTER 24

The tale Miss Lilly told me was about the time she was working long hours for the Senate Agriculture Committee at the Capitol. The piddling pay didn't even cover her rent. She loved the job anyway because she got to work on stuff she thought was important, stuff she thought made a difference.

That was until she found a sealed envelope on her desk with a note from her boss scrawled on the outside. When she saw what was inside, she got so hot under the collar that she did what she always did when she needed space to think. She grabbed her car keys and started driving. By the time she got to Lantz she knew it would be a mistake to go to her daddy with the story. He'd told her that seeing her working in the Legislature made up for her choosing UT over A&M. That's why she stormed into the Store instead of going home.

"Sara was getting ready to close when I charged in. I pitched the envelope on the counter and asked her if all men were cockroaches or just the ones I worked for?"

Lilly said she was so distracted she didn't even notice a wide-eyed Katie Brooks sitting at the counter about ready to eat an overstuffed ham and cheese. Katie was in her last weeks of high school. Sara told Katie to get on with her dinner and locked the front door of the Store.

"I can't remember Sara's exact words, but it was something about the reason a cliché becomes a cliché is because it fits so many dang moments. She said it was at times like these ol' Jimmy Buffett would counsel us to remember, 'It's five o'clock somewhere.' Then she produced a bottle of Jim Beam from under the counter."

Lilly and Sara enjoyed a little Kentucky bourbon while they contemplated the envelope and its contents. Inside was an inch-and-a-half sheet metal screw. Scrawled on the outside of the envelope in Lilly's boss's handwriting were the words, "I'd like to discuss possibilities with you."

Sara finished off her whiskey and pitched the envelope aside. "Not too subtle, is he?"

Katie, who'd been sitting quietly next to them picked it up, looking from the screw to the words written on the envelope.

"Holy Moley," she said. "You don't mean?"

"Are you going to quit?" Sara asked.

"Thing is I like my job," I told her.

"Then don't quit."

"Masterful synopsis of two unacceptable options. Perhaps I should take him up on his clever attempt at seduction. Damn near irresistible, don't you think?"

"A girl's heart positively goes all aflutter when a man uses hardware to make a play for her affection," Sara said, filling the glasses.

"Score one point for originality, then take away seven for crudeness. Wonder if he used props to propose to his wife?"

Lilly said she noticed Katie trying to hide a brown paper wrapped package on the seat next to her.

"What you got there, kiddo? Want to share?"

"Not really," Katie responded, tears starting to fill her eyes.

Lilly said it must have been the whiskey or maybe her black mood, but she pushed Katie to show them what was in the package. When Sara left to fetch Katie a piece of pecan pie for dessert, she grabbed the package and tore it open. Katie was mortified, and Lilly said she felt like a creep. Inside was a lacquered pine board with a corncob nailed to it. Someone had attached an engraved plaque to it. The plaque read: "Presented to Katie Sue Brooks who walks like she has a cob up her butt."

When Sara returned and demanded an explanation, Katie told them that she got an anonymous note to expect a surprise at school today. Because she'd done a load of volunteer computer work for the 4-H Club during the year she thought maybe it would be a Thank You Certificate or the like during the school honor's assembly.

"I even wore my second-best Sunday dress," Katie said, her voice breaking up as she explained her excitement. "I waited but they didn't call my name during the assembly. I found that plaque in my locker after."

"Good God Almighty, Honeydew. And I thought I was having a bad day."

Sara asked Katie if she knew who'd thought up such a nasty prank and Katie said she suspected it might be Rusty Pritchett.

"Isn't he that scrawny little pissant that works at the gas station?" Sara replied. "His daddy's always been useless as tits on a boar. What makes you think of him?"

Katie said since Rusty couldn't afford a computer she sometimes met up with him in the library to let him use her laptop. She overheard some boys teasing him about her being his girlfriend and all.

"He said, 'no way.' I was too fat and walked funny and smelled funny," Katie said.

"And that, Ray, is how a pissant becomes a full-grown cockroach."

I had listened to Miss Lilly's story without interruption, but I was having trouble following exactly where she thought it was leading me and I told her so.

"The point I'm trying to make, Ray, is that Sara is the kind of person you can take your troubles to. She helps people. She told us that when someone messes with you, you have two choices. You can either get mad or get even. She said getting mad was a waste of energy. Getting even, on the other hand, could be quite satisfying."

Her story was finally starting to make some sense.

"You remember what Sara did to Kyle?" Lilly asked.

"Hell, everyone for three counties around knows what she did to Kyle and their double-wide after he cheated on her. She gave a whole new meaning to the term 'mobile home.'"

Both of us took a minute to enjoy the mental image and chuckle a bit.

Lilly said Sara's idea was not to physically injure the other person.

"You need to send a message," she said.

"What kind of message?"

"You have their number and they can't mess with you."

"Tit for tat."

"There were rules though. No innocents should be harmed in the process when you exact your revenge. No 'collateral damage,' as she called it. She said the size of the hurt should fit the size of the inflicted pain. And, finally, revenge should have a bit of wit to it when possible."

"Interesting set of rules. What did you do?"

Lilly said she wasn't sure she should tell me in case they broke a law. I promised her I had bigger fish to fry.

The "screw master," as she referred to her state senator boss, was overly fond of his boathouse on Lake Austin. He bragged about it and often threw big shindigs for his snobby friends. Sara said it was perfect. They decided to sneak in when Miss Lilly knew he would be tied up on the Senate floor. They piled the contents of several boxes of screws on the blades of the ceiling fans the senator had installed over the bar. The next time he turned on the fans, screws would fly over the heads of his buddies like they were under attack by a Gatlin gun.

"He'd get the message all right," Miss Lilly said.

"What about the Pritchett boy?"

"He fancied himself a mechanic. Like a lot of men, he didn't like to ask for directions or read instructions. Thought he knew everything there was to know. Made it easy," Lilly said. The boy just happened to have a run-down motorbike he was forever tinkering with.

"It was an oil burner. We shoved a corncob deep into the exhaust pipe," she explained. "When the bike wouldn't start up, Rusty began taking the engine apart piece by piece. He was so cocksure he would find the problem he never once looked up the exhaust pipe."

"Did he ever figure it out?"

"One of his brothers did. Asked him if he knew how corncob got up into the pipe. Of course, he acted like he didn't have a clue. He got the message though. He knew."

Lilly got up and stretched and walked over to the tiny metal window that had a view out the back of Buster's trailer. I don't see how she could see anything out of the window since it was covered with years' worth of grime. I had the impression her focus was two miles away, so the dirt on the window didn't count for much.

"They are different, Mama and Sara. I quit my job, came back to Lantz and started working with Daddy. Mama wouldn't let go of it. All these years she kept on ragging on me. I never finish any-thing. I'm spoiled. I lack focus. I have no vision or drive. I am going to be an Old Maid. She chewed and chewed on me."

"Did you ever tell her what happened? Why you left Austin?"

"Hell no. She would have found a way to turn it around on me. She had a way of convincing me that I intentionally tried to attract men's attention. She would have had a heyday with that screw business."

Lilly turned around and her eyes were moist with tears. "I don't, you know. Intentionally. Besides if Daddy ever found out he would have...I don't know . . . I couldn't take a chance."

She came back and sat on the bed, rolling the rubber band off another stack of letters.

"Sara knew how to get back at people who did nasty things."

"You're telling me this because you want me to know how far Sara will go to exact revenge?"

"Yes, sir," Lilly said with emphasis. Then as if realizing how her answer might sound, she quickly back peddled. "Look here, Ray. Sara may have written the book on revenge, but she would never, I say, *never* do anything to cause anyone physical harm. That's why I know she'd never hurt Mama the way someone did. That's not Sara's way."

Lilly unfolded the top letter in the new stack and read it slowly before letting out a low whistle and handing it to me.

"Holy crap."

CHAPTER 25

Miss Belle and Buster had planned a secret rendezvous in Hawaii.

Dearest B,

The ticket arrived!!! It was clever of you to send the ticket in the same package with the service patches our Methodist Youth Fellowship is collecting for the display at the Florence VFW Hall.

Daddy is soooo clueless. Mama still makes me nervous. Sometimes I think she is reading my mind. It really creeps me out. I didn't let on when I saw who the package was from, even though I was so excited I almost couldn't eat supper. If they think it is part of our church's pen pal ministry with our boys in uniform, they pay it no mind. Little do they know. Ha. Ha.

I have a final exam when I get back to ETSU campus tomorrow so I can't write much tonight. I haven't told them I won't be returning next semester so no sense studying toooo hard. Ha. Ha. I promise to send a long letter soon!

Hugs and kisses,
Your Belle.

My Dear B,

My parents are soooo stupid. They actually believe I'm going to Florida with my cousin over the break. She is a dream to help cover for me. I will find a way to repay her.

I spent a long time at the library yesterday looking up information about Hawaii. Did you know there are only 12 letters in the Hawaiian alphabet? How can they possibly create enough words to talk to each other? Bizarro!

I felt all grown up when I received the information you sent from the Army that explained the procedures when I arrive at Fort DeRussy for your R&R. The Army must have code names for everything. Fancy calling a vacation "Rest & Recuperation"? I really feel as if I'm part of the war effort. Like the USO.

Would you laugh at me if I told you I've never been out of Texas and I'm a little scared? The thought of flying that many miles makes me shake inside. I've always dreamed of leaving Lantz for somewhere far away and now it's really, really happening.

Stay sweet. It won't be long until I see you.

Your ever-loving, Belle

P.S. Your last letter said we would be staying at the Hilton Rainbow Towers on Waikiki Beach. I guess I shouldn't have to ask. I want to make sure we will each have our own room. Right?

Hello Hello,

You won't believe all the cute clothes I've found to bring on the trip. Mama took me to the Hancock Mall in Austin to shop. Of course, she thinks I'm going to Florida with my cousin. Ha. Ha. Ha.

I pray you will like my swimsuit. It is a two-piece. I had a big fight with Mama over it. She thinks it shows too much skin. I had to show her there were plenty of others on the rack that were much less ladylike. She finally gave in. I knew she would if I stuck to my guns. When I want something, I want it! I won't say any more because I want you to be surprised.

Your Aggie buddies are back in town for the summer and they've hooked back up with that lazy boy from school, Ray Osborne, who all of you used to run around with. Did you know Ray went to the University of Texas on scholarship? Bobby S. and Blake T. give him no end of trouble for choosing UT instead of A&M. Someone at church told me Ray joined the National Guard. Or maybe it was the Army Reserve. I can never tell them apart. It doesn't matter because he's not a real soldier like you.

Counting the days,
Belle

We'd only read a few letters in the final stack when we heard Bobby and Ed pull up.

"Let's clear this up," Lilly said, grabbing up the letters. "I think this is too much for Ed right now."

"I'll tend to this. You go see what they found out at the funeral home."

After Lilly left, I stacked away the letters we'd already sorted but kept out those with the latest postmarks that I wanted to read. I closed the trunk and slid it back under Buster's bed before joining everyone outside in the front yard.

Bobby had his hat in one hand and his other on Ed's shoulder, talking directly at him. "I mean it. You have to let me do this for Buster."

When he heard me, Bobby turned around and included me in the conversation. "Help me out here, Ray. I'm trying to convince Ed to let me help with the funeral. I want to do it for old times' sake. For Buster."

"How did things go over in Killeen?" I asked Ed.

"You wouldn't believe how much it costs," he said. "The VA helps some but it's not much. Only the plot and marker."

"The four of us go way back," Bobby said. "We look after each other. Let me do this."

Ed stared at Miss Lilly with a lost look, and although she didn't say a word, she seemed to give him the answer he needed. He shook Bobby's hand in genuine gratitude. "Thank you, man. I owe you."

Bobby gave Ed a buddy hug and said, "My pleasure. I'll get out of the way to let you folks finish things."

I followed Bobby to his truck. After he got in, he rolled down his window and I stood there shuffling my feet a bit.

"Damn nice of you to help," I told him.

"Shame about Buster. When do you think they will know what happened?" he replied.

"Hard to tell. Hard to tell," I said because I didn't want to take the conversation where I knew it needed to go. I shuffled some more and finally got to the point. I told him I had something to discuss with him if he would be home later.

He smiled in that Bobby carefree way and said, "Any time, my friend," before pulling away. That smile crawled up my back and stung me like a spider bite since I knew our relationship would most likely change after I talked to him about what I had to talk to him about.

Back inside the trailer, Miss Lilly and Ed were sitting at the tiny dining table holding hands.

"It was nice of Bobby," Lilly said.

"He's a nice man," I said joining them.

I had to ask Ed about guns, so I jumped in. I explained that the gun the Austin folks took with them wasn't the Browning High Power 9mm Buster had threatened me with a while back. The one that had apparently ended Buster's life was covered in blood but was a Colt.

"What's your question?" Ed responded in a noncommittal way.

"I was wondering if you could tell me what happened to the Browning and what other firearms you and your uncle keep around."

Ed scratched his head and looked confused.

"Ray, I can't help you. I had my fill of guns in the service. Told my uncle I had no use for them and didn't want them around the place. As far as I know he sold the Browning. I don't know anything about a Colt."

I made a note of what he told me. One more thing added to my long list of things to check. I pulled out the Chevron service station receipt and asked him if he was the one who had bought the Drumstick and beef jerky. He looked it over and said the credit card was Buster's.

"If you're about done with questions, I'd like to get us something to eat," Miss Lilly said.

"Almost done for now," I answered. "I will need to follow up about the safe deposit box and next steps on Buster's estate."

"It's too early to settle anything. Thank God we're caught up on taxes and the mortgage. I'll stay here for a while. I should be able to manage until I can sort things out."

I arranged a time to meet Ed at the bank to peek at the contents of Buster's safe deposit box. Lilly asked if I wanted to join them at the Store for a bite to eat. I explained I had a few things I still needed to document for my police report. With Ed's permission I would remain there and take a few snapshots for the record. The beauty of a small town like Lantz is neither of them thought it was at all strange to have the local sheriff nosing around.

"Make yourself at home," Ed said as he left.

"I'll lock up when I leave," I promised.

What I wanted was to get my hands on the colored photo of Diamondhead. As I suspected, when I pulled it from the frame, it was a postcard. Nothing was written on the back of the postcard, but behind it was a set of faded black and white photos of Buster and Belle. One beach photo was of their bare feet cuddled next to each other. Another was of Buster holding Belle's hand. They were in a pineapple field. On her finger was a large coral ring. R.W. was right about her hands. I put the Diamondhead postcard back in the plastic frame and hung it on the wall. I pocketed the pictures along with Belle's letters that I still needed to read.

I locked up and drove to Bobby's place. It was not a conversation I relished.

CHAPTER 26

The iced tea was just as cold and the view just as sweet as it was the last time we sat on Bobby's back porch. Wish I could say as much about my frame of mind. Once I filled Bobby in on the FBI meeting, he hurled a full glass of tea against the wall. I was grateful to be out of firing range.

"God damn, son of a bitch to hell and back," he barked. That was mighty strong language coming out of Bobby's mouth. Maybe the strongest I'd ever heard him utter.

"Do you want to consult a lawyer before we talk anymore?"

"How can they do that, Ray? What kind of country do we live in when they can record the private conversations of a tax-paying citizen? Is this Russia or something?"

"A lawyer can explain all of it to you."

"You know the law. You explain it," he said, running his hand over his bald head in frustration.

"They had a warrant, Bobby. Looks like it was all by the book. They've been investigating a group of lobbyists, lawmakers, and other crooks tied to some shady dealings with members of the Cattlemen's Board. You got caught in their trap."

"Makes me feel like a mess of fried horse turds."

"You're small potatoes. They think they almost have enough to make a case for some big-time corruption. That's why they're offering a deal."

"What kind of deal?"

I told him I wasn't up on all the particulars. I understood they wanted to set up a sting operation. He would wear a recording device. Perhaps there would be hidden cameras at the meet up. Bobby would likely have a bunch of marked cash he would offer in exchange for a favor. The feds would get it all on tape. If he worked with the feds, they wouldn't charge him for the "little indiscretion" they'd already recorded.

"They'll exchange your cooperation for leniency," I said.

"Jesus H. Christ," Bobby said, dropping back into his seat and plowing his head with both hands. "They want me to rat out the fellas to save my own skin."

"Pretty much. Hell of a deal," I replied.

"How much time do I have?"

Because of the logistics involved, the FBI would need a fast answer. I told Bobby I could probably buy him some time to think it over and discuss it with a lawyer.

"More than a few days and they will likely withdraw the deal," I explained.

Bobby went into the kitchen to fetch a dustpan and broom. I sipped iced tea while he cleaned up the mess he'd made. When he was finished, I decided it was time to loosen the laces and drop the other shoe.

"We need to talk about how all this fits into the night Miss Belle died."

"If you've got more talking to do, I'm going to need something stronger than tea. Excuse me."

He returned with a beer and popped the top.

"Shoot," he said, taking a long drink from a cold Shiner.

"When we talked about Monica's ashes, you said you and Miss Belle argued. We both know that was only part of it. Let's go back over the story again. I want to be sure of the details before you talk to your lawyer and before you talk to the feds. Let's start with the note you wrote her."

Bobby studied the beer bottle for a while. "I didn't kill her."

"Nobody said you did. I'm telling you that you need to be clear about everything that happened."

"Like I told you, I blew my stack. I was hurt but I didn't kill her."

"So you said."

"I was ready to have it out with her. I put the note on the screen door before I left for Austin early Sunday morning. Blake wasn't home and the place was silent and dark. Don't think Belle was up yet. Belle called back and left a message inviting me to come by. I drove back to Lantz to talk to her in the afternoon. When I got there, she had sandwiches and mimosas laid out on the sideboard in the dining room. Invited me in and filled a plate like I was one of her lady friends who'd dropped in for an afternoon chat and chew. I can't imagine what she was thinking. I didn't want any part of it," Bobby said. "I was pretty hot under the collar."

"Did you get physical?"

"No. Certainly not. How can you ask that?"

"They will ask."

"Okay."

"What did you say?"

"When I challenged her, she came right back at me. She said I was the one disrespecting Monica because I didn't follow her wishes by taking her remains to Maryland."

"How did that make you feel?"

"It was like a slap in the face. You know how Belle is . . .was. Talking to her sometimes was like trying to explain magic tricks to a dog. No matter what you say you know it's just wasted words. The stuff she said about Monica and me not respecting her wishes. I don't usually have trouble knowing what to say but she cold cocked me."

I could see his quandary. Bobby without a good comeback is practically uncharted territory.

"Truth is, I'm not sure she even noticed. She started slurring her words and said something about getting back at me for bidding on a pineapple cake or some such nonsense. That's when I realized that Belle was starting to act sleepy and when she tried to stand up to refill her glass, she was wobbly and nearly stumbled. I figured she'd had one too many mimosas. I practically had to carry her upstairs. I laid her out on her bed and pulled a cover over her."

"That was after three o'clock?"

"Best as I recall. She was passed out cold. But she was definitely alive when I went back to Austin for that other meeting."

"You drove straight to Austin from her house?"

"Like I told you, I try to beat the rush hour traffic. Stopped in at the Driskill. I had a room reserved but decided not to spend the night after all so I checked out. There were still a lot of Association members milling about. You know how it goes. Got to talking and I still needed to go by that other meeting. After I dropped in there, I left Austin. Got home in time to tuck in for the night. Long fucking day."

I made some notes and stood to go, extending my hand to Bobby.

"When you talk to the feds, make sure your attorney is with you, Bobby. This is serious shit," I urged him. "Don't put it off."

Driving away from his house, I could see Bobby in my rearview mirror. He was standing at his front door with a hangdog expression, as if he couldn't decide whether to go inside or take a ride. A conversation like the one we'd just had could leave a man in a state like that.

The Driskill Hotel had confirmed his check-out time at after four o'clock. It would be easy to check his alibi with other Association members. He was taped by the Feds at around seven, around the period the DPS medical examiner says someone was putting an end to Miss Belle's life. Looks like he had one hell of an ironclad alibi for her murder. I had some sorting out to do before confronting the others on my shrinking list of suspects.

CHAPTER 27

The General Store was closed, so I drove up the road where I found Blake's truck parked at Sara's house. She opened the door before I knocked.

"Saw you drive up," she said. "Come on in."

When I hesitated, she snickered. "Don't worry, Twizy's with Mama in her bedroom and the door's shut."

Blake was nursing a cold beer and didn't seem especially glad to see me. Blake being Blake, he offered me something to drink anyway. I had to decline.

"Business," I said.

"Course it is." His lip ticked up around the edge like he had a bitter taste in his mouth.

Sara curled up in her spot on the couch, tucking her legs under her and organizing her pillow fort around her. "Give him a break, Blake. This will all be over soon. It's time we get things sorted out."

Sara pointed to the only empty seat in the place and I took it, pulling out my notepad and flipping around for an empty page.

"I'm here about Buster and what the three of you talked about on the night Belle died."

Sara and Blake studied each other. Neither said a word.

"Okay. I see how it's going to be," I said. "Here's what I know, Blake. You came back early from the Cattlemen's Association meeting in Austin, but you didn't go home. You came to Sara's house. Don't deny it. I watched Hattie Mae brush Twizy hair off your trousers the next morning. You want to explain?"

"What's your point?" Sara asked with enough sass to set the chip on her shoulder to rocking.

"My point is that the two of you haven't given me a straight answer about how things played out on the night someone killed Miss Belle, and I have a murder to solve. A murder, I might add, that the DPS is trying to pin on you, my friend," I said, making eye contact with Blake. "I'd say it is in everyone's interest to quit playing around and lay your cards on the table."

"My lawyer would say I shouldn't let the law try to talk to me if she isn't here," Blake said.

"Well, I'd say she's absolutely, one hundred percent right," I replied, getting up and dusting cat hair off my trousers with my hat. "Let's call her and set an appointment."

My hand was on the screen door when he spoke.

"Hellfire and damnation from here to Mississippi," Blake said with a sigh that sounded like he was letting the air out of a truck tire. "Guess it's about time to either fish or cut bait. Come back and sit down, Ray," he said as he got up and moved next to Sara on the couch, taking her hand in his and looking at it as if he was seeing it for the first time. Then he kissed her, first on the cheek and then on each eye as if he was saying something to her in a language only the two of them understood.

He stayed there, next to her and then motioned to me to take the chair he'd vacated.

"Better sit down. This may take a little while. Sure you don't want something to drink?"

I may have mentioned Blake had never been a big talker. When he started in, I swear to you, it was as if a powerful verbal laxative had been administered to an oral obstruction

His story began in high school, when he first loved Sara but married Belle.

"You know how things are when you're young," he said. "I had to do right by Belle when she told me she was in the family way. I did my dead level best to make her happy and give her everything she asked for. Trouble is, I don't think she knew what she wanted."

"Belle was too much like her Mama. Doris, that was her name, was one of those prickly women who started talking the minute she came in a room, moving around picking up things and putting them down again. Asked a lot of questions without waiting for an answer. "

"Mama had a saying that I always felt fit Doris," Sara said. "She was like a drum. Tight, empty, and only good for making noise."

Blake explained that Doris was a California transplant who moved in with her uncle, an East Texas dairy farmer with limited means and a big heart, after her father walked out on the family. Sixteen-year-old Doris found herself transported from manicures and embroidered poodle skirts in a Los Angeles suburb to a rural schoolhouse sitting next to barefoot farm boys in overalls. When the local kids tried to strike up a conversation in the lunchroom, she'd pinch up her nose and move to another table. In a day or two they quit trying to make friends with the snooty girl from the West Coast.

Doris cried herself to sleep at night, and it wasn't long before she was refusing to go to classes, pretending to be sick. Her aunt, who dipped snuff and had a cackle for a laugh, introduced Doris around her Baptist church. Doris wouldn't even taste the food at Wednesday night covered dish suppers because she said it "smelled funny." Before long she was losing weight at a frightening clip.

Her mother and aunt were beside themselves when one weekend old friends from Lantz came for visit. Their son, an upper classman at Texas A&M, made a beeline for Doris, who he found glamorous in her California garb. Before the visit was over, Doris and the Aggie had packed up his father's car and eloped to Las Vegas. By morning she was a married woman. Doris's aunt and uncle didn't have children. That's why they left their acreage in Bowie County to Doris. She couldn't sell it off fast enough after they passed.

"By then Doris was a widow. It fell to me to drive her back to East Texas to settle her aunt and uncle's affairs," Blake said. "That old lady didn't stop complaining from the time her head lifted off the pillow until she closed her eyes at night. The food. The people. The smells. Aches and pains. Politics. You name it."

Blake said he'd done a little reading up on local history before going to Bowie County and learned that the country schoolhouse that Doris had talked about in such a hateful way had a beautiful history.

"What tugged at my heart was the story of the farmer who'd donated the legacy land and materials used to build the school during the Depression. He wanted to make sure it was the kind of place where farm children could feel at home in their overalls."

Local men cleared the land and used simple hand tools to construct the sturdy school building. With its native stone, floor-to-ceiling windows, and striking pine wood floors the school is, even today, a testament to Texas craftsmanship.

"That was the problem with Doris. She missed what was worth caring about by talking quick and judging fast," Blake said. "She passed all that along to Belle in the way she raised her. Judgmental. Stuck up. Hot-tempered. Spiteful."

I was jotting a few notes as Blake talked and hated like hell to interrupt him now that he was finally on a roll, but for the life of me I couldn't see how talking about Doris was getting us to my point about the night Belle died. I told Blake as much.

"Sorry 'bout that, Ray. When Buster showed up, you're right about that by the way, it just so happens Sara and I had been having a quiet evening, talking about Belle and Doris and how proud I was that Lilly didn't take after her Grandma Doris. My Lilly is tough and independent and fearless, but she's full of heart. Not like Belle," Blake said. "Here I was talking about Belle the way I was and she was all alone on her last night on this earth. I don't know how I'll ever be able to . . ."

Blake stopped talking for a while and I thought the spigot might have cut off again but he took a deep breath and started up again.

"She can't help the way she was because of how she was raised," he said.

"I guess that's true for us all," I offered.

"So anyway," he said. "About then Buster shows up, banging on the door, four sheets to the wind."

"Got Twizy all stirred up and Buster paid for it," Sara added.

"I saw the wounds on his hands," I told her. "Tony, over at The Rattlesnake, confirms Buster spent the afternoon with his VFW boys, day drinking."

"Night drinking, too. Buster was an ugly drunk, I don't have to tell you," Blake said.

Sara said she tried to fix him something to eat and told him he'd have to tone it down because Grace Lawrence was resting.

"He was having none of it," she said.

"Can't tell you what got into him," Blake said. "I know he was packing a whole boatload of grief and bitterness. Before you know it, he's telling me all kinds of crazy stuff about him and Belle when he was a soldier. I let him carry on because he's mostly talking out of his head until he claimed I wasn't Lilly's real dad. That's when I lost it."

"What happened?"

"I hit him in the stomach. Knocked the wind out of him and sent him to the floor."

Sara picked up the story. She explained that she sent Blake out of the house for a walk while she cleaned up where Buster tossed his cookies. After he'd sipped on some water and could breathe a little, she gave him a wet towel for his head. She wanted Buster to leave before Blake got back from his walk but figured he needed to sober up some more first. She went to the kitchen to brew coffee and fix something to eat. When she returned Buster had found her whiskey stash and was drinking straight from the bottle.

"Blake walked in and they took out after each other again," Sara said.

"Buster wouldn't let it go. He told me I had to keep Lilly from marrying Ed because they were cousins and would give me mongrel grandchildren," Blake said. "He also starting ragging about R.W. and how Belle had been grooming him to be the perfect son-in-law until she found out he was queer. Said Lilly sure could pick 'em. Called her a 'cousin fucker,' and some other slurs I couldn't quite make out."

"Before I could stop it Blake was threatening to kill Buster," Sara said.

"Is that when Buster left here?" I asked.

"You mean, is that when I threw him out?" Sara asked. "Truth be told, I don't think he even remembered later what he said. I'm pretty sure he wasn't in his right mind."

"That's no excuse, is it?" I asked.

"I've seen him that way before and usually I ignore it," Blake said. "I won't let him go after Lilly. That crosses a line with me."

"You know that I've got to ask," I said looking at Blake. "You said that you threatened to kill him."

"Now you want to know if I did. Seems I have a pretty good alibi since your buddy had me in custody when Buster died."

"I had to ask."

"Curious job you have, my friend."

Sara gave me a side glance and asked, "Do you think Buster was murdered, too? I heard he'd shot himself."

I told her from what it looked like at the scene the experts from Austin were assuming he'd committed suicide. However, they were withholding a final ruling until they'd completed the postmortem.

"They're likely right but I'm not ready to say one way or the other because we didn't find a note. A one-horse town like Lantz goes decades without a suspicious death and then we get two in the same week. I'm saying you only see a coincidence like that in cheap detective novels."

CHAPTER 28

The First United Methodist Church of Lantz was doing their darnedest for Miss Belle's last hurrah. Floral arrangements, whose fragrance was so strong it overpowered the first three rows of the sanctuary, and easels heavy with sprays of flowers filled the altar and flowed down the side aisles. The steps leading up to the altar and surrounding the ornate mahogany coffin were crowded with baskets of green plants. The casket blanket had so many yellow roses I felt certain they'd had to empty flower markets in several towns just to meet the specifications.

The preacher said all the usual things preachers say at such a time, reading from John 14:2 about a place prepared in heaven and summarizing Miss Belle's life and her dedication to the church. He didn't mention how she'd died. He stumbled a bit when he offered up a reminder that every good Methodist is admonished by John Wesley to do all the good you can, by all the means you can, in all the ways you can, in all the places you can, at all the times you can, for as long as you can. He recovered his footing when he eased into preaching about the Good Lord's gift of prevenient grace and looked genuinely relieved to relinquish the microphone when he called on Miss Lilly to say a few words.

Miss Lilly was on the front row sitting between her daddy and Ed. As she stood, she motioned for R.W. to join her and they walked hand in hand to the pulpit.

"As most of you know, Mama raised R.W. and me together, like brother and sister," she said. "I can't imagine anyone who Mama would rather have part of her final service than my brother of the heart."

Lilly unfolded a piece of paper and smoothed it out in front of her on the lectern. "I've written some words here, but none of them seem to fit my feelings about Mama and how things ended. I suppose the Germans have a word for how I feel. Or maybe the French. They have words for feelings that we don't have in English," Lilly said.

"Our language is great for naming things. It's not always as good at supplying the exact word to express a mixed-up emotion or strange feeling or complex circumstance. That's why our authors devote paragraphs upon paragraphs to descriptions of what it feels like when a lover cheats on you or your cat dies or, against all odds, you win a race.

"To say Mama was complicated seems altogether inadequate. She was blunt, to be sure. She was also strong and determined. She got things done. Look around this church. How much of what you see is here because of her grit?"

Lilly paused and let the folks in the congregation survey the sanctuary and absorb appreciation for the point she made.

"She had secrets and unfulfilled dreams I never knew about because she didn't talk about them. She locked them away in a place for lost longings and what might have been."

Lilly stopped when her voice quivered. She took a deep breath and soldiered on.

"What might have been. Now that is as raw an idea as any person can utter. And crazy sad, too. I wish she had shared her dreams with me. I wish I had known about her sister who died all those years ago. I wish I had known her as a fresh-faced young woman with plans to travel the world.

"The day after she died, I heard some people from this very church talking about her. Some of the things they said were not kind. Maybe if they had known these things about her, they would have been less quick to judge. She may have earned some of those words, but she didn't deserve to have someone steal her life from her. Someone needs to answer for that."

The sanctuary was punctuated with nervous coughing and a woman in the back, which sounded like Katie Sue Brooks, started to hiccough. Miss Lilly's face was turning pale when she stepped back and gave the microphone to R.W. It was his turn.

R.W. held Miss Lilly's hand while he talked. His voice was strong and direct, but he managed a gentle tone.

"The chance to really know Miss Belle has passed for all of us now. Maybe the greatest gift she gave us was a lesson about how difficult people are often carrying heartaches and what-might-have-beens. She was a builder, a doer, a mother to a boy who lost his own at a tender age, a lover of old movies, a perfectionist who had a way with bougainvillea, and a woman who dressed every day in preparation for what life would send her," he said, pausing to take a breath. "One of her favorite expressions was, 'You shouldn't leave the house without your spurs on because you never know when you'll meet a horse.' I like to imagine her now, dressed to the nines, spurs on, ready for whatever is coming her way."

You could feel the mood lighten ever so slightly. The tension the mourners had held unconsciously in their jaws for days loosened like a wave of relief, spreading from pew to pew. In a town such as Lantz where everyone knows everyone, funerals come and go. To attend one for a woman who died the way Miss Belle died, where your neighbors and friends are suspects, had put pressure on the good graces of the entire community. The collective release when they'd made it through the service without incident was almost audible.

Recorded music began playing, and the song was *Keep Me in Your Heart for A While*. R.W. and Lilly returned to their seats. Ushers directed a ceremonial procession of mourners past Miss Belle's coffin, where she was laid out in a high-buttoned tomato-colored suit that matched the rose tones painted on her cheeks. Some folks stopped to shake hands with Blake and Miss Lilly on the front pew. I was one of them.

I spoke softly in Miss Lilly's ear. "You done your mama proud." The look she gave me in return told me we'd be okay. When I got to Blake, I started to shake his hand and then, from a place I didn't know I even owned, I grabbed him in a bear hug that seemed to surprise him as much as it did me.

"I promise you I'll get to the bottom of this."

He hugged me back.

"You do that, Ray. You do that."

CHAPTER 29

I decided to skip the graveside services and reception for Miss Belle. S.W. was on the Ladies' Auxiliary committee for arrangements and would represent us. I needed to go back to the office and relieve my deputy, who never likes to miss a free meal. Besides, I had work to do.

After Johnnie Lake cleared out, I spread out the photos I'd taken from under the Diamondhead postcard at Buster's place. Then I read Belle's final letters that I had separated out from those we'd found in Buster's trunk. They were the last ones she'd written to him after she'd returned from Hawaii.

Hello Sweetheart,

I feel it is okay now to call you Sweetheart after all that happened in Hawaii. I am all grown up now. When I close my eyes, I get all tingly. I can hear the ocean waves and feel the sand on our toes.

It's nothing like the nasty Texas beaches. The sand at Padre Island is like sludge and the Gulf smells of dead things and oil. In Hawaii the waves pound against you and you can brush the sand off your feet with your hand. Heaven!!! Mama and Daddy have no idea where I've been. They think my tan is from Florida! Ha. Ha.

I am still worried about how you looked way too thin. I thought the Army did a better job of feeding our boys in uniform. You asked me not to write my Congressman. I won't if you promise to try to put on some weight. I worry about you. You must stay strong for the fight.

I hope you like the pictures I took of the two of us on the beach. I loved the way my toes looked with fresh polish. Did you like the red? I think I will wear red polish on my toes from now on to help me remember Hawaii. Do I sound decadent?

Your little moustache made you look soooo mature and, even though you didn't like it, I think the aloha shirt was cute on you. So there!

Love,

Belle

P.S. I am trying to get the HEB in Georgetown to start carrying fresh pineapple. I've already talked to the manager. It was sooooo good when they would slice it open right there in the field. I worry that it is bad for a girl's figure. But it is sooooo good. Ha. Ha.

Hello Sweet Buster,

Guess what? I contacted a bunch of airlines about how to become a stewardess. After Hawaii I know I will never be happy in Lantz.

My Grandma used to tell me I needed to find my special spot. And, Buster, that's my spot. Up in the air, seeing the world! Can you believe it? I owe it all to you.

Come fly with me?

Belle

P.S. Which uniform do you like the best? American Airlines, Delta or Southwest? I can't decide.

Hello Soldier Boy,

There's big news around town. Bobby S. came back from a fraternity trip to Our Nation's Capital with a wife on his arm. Can you believe it? Her name is Monica. She's a tiny little thing with frizzy hair and blue eyes.

She dresses funny and talks real strange. I can't imagine what he was thinking. She's not one of us. Mama invited her to dinner right after she settled in and Monica asked us to explain fried okra. You don't mean. Can anyone be so completely stupid?

Bobby's totally smitten. He's building a huge house out on the Austin highway. With his daddy's money no less. So much space for just the two of them. Monica's a showoff if you ask me. Laughing all the time and cooking up Northern dishes that have no spices to speak of. I ask you, who's ever heard of slippery noodles? What is the world coming to?

Got to run. I'm late for Wednesday night Fellowship at the church. I promise to write a longer letter soon.

Hugs and kisses,

Your Belle

P.S. I pray for you every chance I get. There was a song in services on Sunday that made me think of you and the way you were so scared sometimes in your sleep. It was about praying to God to defend us from the fears and terrors of the night and saving us from a troubled, restless sleep. I don't remember all the words but I'm going to look it up and make a copy of it from the hymnal and send it to you if I can find it.

The final letter looked as if it had been manhandled. It was wrinkled as if someone had waded in a ball but later smoothed it back out. There was a wide gap in the date from the letter with news about Bobby and Monica and the final letter to Buster.

Dear Buster,
    This will be my last letter to you. Blake Tackett has asked me to marry him and I have accepted his proposal. We have plans for renovation of his family home place. He is the kind of man who will provide a good home for me. We hope to have a family really soon. I will continue to pray for your safe return from war.
    Sincerely,
    Veda

The dates on the final letter took me back in time. Those were hectic weeks. I was enrolled in classes at UT Austin during the day and working night shifts at a bar on the Drag for extra money. It was pure luck that Blake caught me at home when he showed up unexpectedly at my rat hole apartment late one afternoon to tell me the news. He'd cut classes at A&M. Anyone who knew Blake understood that a trip to Longhorn territory was unheard of. It's only a two-hour drive between the two universities, but we tended to hook up in Lantz to avoid each other's campuses since the UT-A&M rivalry was legendary.

One look at Blake's face and I figured I'd better find us somewhere to talk. My apartment didn't lend itself to such because I shared it with two east coast snobs who asked a lot of questions. Since I was majoring in history with no clear idea of what exactly I would do with a history degree, I tried to avoid prolonged conversations with the boys from Boston. Seems they had some very definite ideas about their own futures: degrees in economics and then on to law school. Big plans for a future in corporate law. I assumed I would wind up teaching back in Lantz. As you might imagine, we didn't have a lot in common. They paid their share of the rent on time, and even in those days, Austin wasn't cheap, so I tried my best not to complain.

My place was a few blocks off main campus, making it only a short walk up the Drag before Blake and I were settled in at a corner booth at the Night Hawk restaurant. We ordered their famous Top Chop't steak, slaw, and fries. While we waited, Blake explained his visit.

"I've asked Belle to marry me."

"Did you say 'Belle'?" I asked, confused. "I thought you and Sara. . . ."

"You see Belle is, you know. Well, we need to, you see."

I drank some iced tea and didn't say anything. I did see. That didn't mean I understood.

"Want you to be my best man."

"No problem. What about Bobby?"

"He's mad at me."

"How so?"

"Complicated."

We ate our chopped steak and followed it up with coconut cream pie. We talked about football and Vietnam and music and roommates and classes and our parents and whatever else we could work in to avoid the obvious question of how Blake found himself about to marry Belle instead of Sara. As he was getting ready to leave, he said the wedding plans were moving fast and I'd be getting information from Belle about the particulars.

"She's got lots of ideas. About colors and flowers and such."

"I'll bet she does."

The wedding was fancy, I'll give Belle credit. Lots of pink as I recall. She and Blake honeymooned in Galveston. It was a quick weekend trip because he couldn't be away from classes for long. She decided to stay in Lantz to begin fixing up the old Tackett family place, and he commuted home on weekends.

It was only a few weeks after the wedding that I had another surprise visitor at my door. It was Belle. She was all dressed up in a fancy canary yellow suit and had on a bit too much makeup. It couldn't cover the red splotches on her face or her puffy eyes.

"May I come in?" she asked.

"Sure," I replied. "I'm afraid this place isn't fit. Why don't I take you out for a bite to eat or a walk?"

We wound up in the same booth at the Night Hawk. This time we didn't order food. Only iced tea.

"I want to go the ASH cemetery and I don't want to go alone," Belle told me after a long, odd silence. It's the kind of silence life is full of. They are the sort of moments that hang in the air, and you don't fill them because you are waiting for something. It isn't really an empty space so much as something that is full of such powerful anticipation that it takes up all the space.

I don't know what I was expecting her to say, but that wasn't it.

"Sure, I'll go with you."

At the cemetery we easily located grave Number 9H47F near the Woodmen of the World marker. I backed off a few steps when Belle knelt down. I wasn't sure if she was crying or praying. After a bit she pulled a blue plush bunny with pink and yellow ears from her purse and sat it on the marker. She stood up, wrapped her arms around her middle, and turned to me.

"We can go now, Ray. What's done is done."

CHAPTER 30

Ed and I had a two o'clock appointment in Killeen where we planned to get a peek inside Buster's safe deposit box. After Ed presented his Power of Attorney and the clerk checked with her boss, they decided to let us open it. I'd like to think my presence and a comment or two to the bank manager about cooperation as opposed to court orders helped to grease the wheels.

The skinny metal bank box contained four documents. The first two were the title to Buster's property and an offer from a pipeline company for an easement across his land. Buster's holographic will left everything to Ed so I figured both would be useful in probate.

The third document was out of the blue. It was another letter from Belle, dated the same day she died. It took me a second to realize it was to Buster since no one addressed him by his given name, Jonathan Francis.

Dear Francis,
I have grown weary of your threats to go to my husband with your mistaken ideas about the "truth" of Lilly's parentage. It has

given me secret pleasure all these years to let you bask in the mis-apprehension you are her father because of our little romp in Hawaii. Enough is enough. If you ever threaten me again, I will turn you over to the law for extortion, harassment and whatever else we can find in the law books. You won't like jail. You should have learned by now not to mess with me.

Veda Tackett

P.S. There is no reason for me to keep these any longer.

Inside the envelope were Belle's trophy rings.

Ed looked at me for an explanation.

"This might get complicated," I said. "What else is in the box?"

He unfolded the last document, gave it a quick once over and shrugged. "Only my adoption papers."

You could have knocked me over with a feather. "Excuse me?"

"Buster's older brother, Harold, and his wife, Susan, adopted me when I was three. Guess he never mentioned it?"

We were standing in the bank vault, and I had to call another audible. Phil might not like it, but I decided I was going to need help untangling the twisted melodrama that lay before me. I figured the best way to do it was to get everyone involved into one place and sort it out together.

* * *

Hattie had set out a buffet of leftovers from the funeral reception and everyone helped themselves to a plate. Food is the one thing there is no shortage of when someone in a small town passes away. It's as if the refrigerator sends a silent dog whistle signal the minute a shelf gets emptied, and sure enough before an hour passes, the doorbell rings and someone delivers more fried chicken, coleslaw, cookies, pie, or cold cuts. The ritual goes on for days.

We gathered at the Tackett kitchen table. That's another thing about small towns. No matter where you set up the spread, people wind up crowded in the kitchen. At some point you need to accept the natural dining instincts of homo sapiens and simply put the food on the kitchen counter to begin with. That's what Hattie had done.

After an hour of eating and sharing stories, Miss Lilly and I had filled everyone in on what we'd learned from Miss Belle's college letters to Buster, including the ones I'd taken back to the office and the photos from behind the Diamondhead postcard.

"I'll return them when this is all over, Ed," I explained.

He shrugged.

Sara and Blake told a sanitized version of what had happened when Buster showed up drunk at her place the night Belle died, and Ed told everyone about the contents of Buster's safe deposit box.

The food and the information took time to digest.

"I've heard a lot about Hawaii over the years. Not all of it, but a lot," Blake said.

"You never said anything to me," Lilly said.

"Nothing to say. Water under the bridge."

"What I don't understand is why Buster would get drunk and insist he was my daddy," Miss Lilly said.

"Maybe he needed to hold on to the lie," I said. "It was like part of him needed to think the lie was true. It was all he had left. If it wasn't true and he let go of that belief, it would finally undo him. The final string would break."

"When she returned the rings, it must have broken his heart," R.W. said.

"Do you think that's what happened? Did he finally break?" Ed asked.

I thought about it before answering.

"It's possible. He was skunk drunk when he left Sara's and he was boiling over," I said. "The bank records show he'd accessed the safe box earlier in the day. That's likely when he put Belle's letter and the rings away."

Miss Lilly was fingering Belle's final correspondence as she spoke. "He never could let any of her letters go. He seems to have kept them all. I think that he couldn't destroy even that last nasty one, but he had to lock it away, out of sight."

I wasn't sure whether to tell them about Belle's singular trip to the ASH cemetery all those years ago. I decided it might be important. When I finished no one reacted except Sara, who stood up, looked at me and then Blake before turning her back on everyone and leaving the room without a word.

Blake started to follow her but Hattie intervened. "You need to give her some space."

No one said much, waiting for Sara to do what she was going to do. Hattie kept our iced tea glasses full and with our help cleared the table and stored the leftovers. It was about half an hour before Sara returned and sat back down.

"Guess I owe you all an explanation," she said without making eye contact with anyone in particular. "I know what caused Belle to go to the cemetery."

Sara explained that she was waiting for her mother, who was on night shift as a LVN at the Georgetown Community Hospital, when Belle came into the emergency room. She was bleeding badly, alone and scared. Miscarriage. She and Blake had only been married a few weeks and he'd already gone back to classes at A&M. Sara held her hand and stayed with her when the doctors ordered a D&C.

"She made me swear not to tell Blake or her mother or anyone. I promised," Sara said. "Guess it doesn't matter now. Problem is it wasn't long after when her unborn child started to haunt me. I had the feeling he—in my imagination it was a boy child—was insisting I acknowledge him. Strange, right?"

"What do you mean by haunt?" Miss Lilly asked.

"At first it was this imaginary image of a precocious baby with curly hair and bubble gum nose. Over time I began to see a wobbly toddler taking his first halting steps. Then a fearless boy riding a tire swing over the river, daring me with his saucy grin. Recently it's been more like a premonition that he's standing in a shadow whenever my heart constricts. More often as not I'll catch his presence in a story I'm reading or in the dust of a dream just before I wake or that faint residue left behind when something stirs my heart."

"Dang woman," Hattie said.

"What do you think it means?" Miss Lilly asked.

Sara turned to Blake and took his hand as if he was the only person in the room.

"I haven't a clue. I do know this. It's a rabbit trail leading to a dead end. It was a phantom, a lie, and it stepped in the way of my heart's desire. That phantom haunting me was a promise I made to Belle to keep a secret. Her secret of an unborn child haunted all our lives: your life, my life, Buster's life, and Lilly's. It even kept Belle from her dreams. It kept us from living our lives the way we were meant to."

By now Sara's eyes were leaking tears and I was afraid everyone in the kitchen was close to joining her. She wasn't finished talking.

"All these years, the truth would have made such a difference, but I promised and I paid the price for keeping that promise. I've spent my life saying, 'do this, then this, then this again.' Then tomorrow comes and then it's next week. Weeks pile on weeks and life and time slips away. Soon it's all gone and the magical 'later' that is promised never comes. Blake, I can't keep chasing 'someday.' Belle's secret caused too much sorrow and lost time. I need to let the phantom go. It's my turn. It's my turn."

CHAPTER 31

If there is majesty in old bones and discount haircuts, it was there in the Patriot Guard stationed along the driveway next to the cemetery shelter where we held Buster's memorial service. The former servicemen had accompanied Buster on their motorcycles, forming an honor guard for the hearse and the scaled-down motorcade that made the short trip from the funeral home to the veteran's cemetery.

Some had turned out in faded Wranglers and ragtag vests, tattooed with brigade patches that spoke of affiliations from long careers. From the respectful way they stood, they may as well have been in full dress blues. All stood with shoulders squared as if in response to a drill sergeant's "atten hut" barked from a half-century past. It was a command easier to obey before arthritis started grinding at their joints and their bellies hung over their belts. Still, they stood their post with dignity because one of theirs had come home and, through his service, had earned their honor and their respect. Once-strong hands held tight to Old Glory as if she relied on them to hold her steady against the wind whipping her back and forth. And maybe, just maybe, she did.

Ed was sitting on the front row with Miss Lilly. R.W., Sara, and Hattie shared the row behind. I noticed some VFW regulars in the rear seats as Katie Sue Brooks arrived, all gussied up with a hat full of flowers that matched her flowered frock. She was holding tight to the hat with one hand—since the wind was trying to blow it from her head—as she waved at me with the other hand. I'd given orders to Deputy Lake to hold down the fort so that Katie could attend. One of these days I'm going to figure out where that man spends all his time. I'd parked my patrol car at a respectful distance and walked a half mile to sit with Bobby and Blake. We were there when this thing started. Seemed fitting we should be together when it ended.

Memory has its way with you at comings and goings. While we waited for services to start, mine drifted back to the four of us, the three B's and me. We were out late one night shortly before graduation our senior year in high school, drinking and talking about the draft. Bobby and Blake were both headed to A&M, which meant that they qualified for a college deferment.

Buster's lottery number was God-awful. His birthday was June 21st. That made his draft number sixty. Bobby and Blake tried to talk Buster into joining them at A&M until he reminded them that he had shit for grades. Besides, he told them, college cost money and his parents couldn't afford it. He told us that since he was a sure shot to be drafted, he'd decided to go ahead and enlist.

"I signed up this afternoon," he said with a shit-eating grin on his face. "You're now looking at one of Uncle Sam's fighting men."

The three of us stared at him, letting the dust settle from the bombshell he'd dropped on us.

"What about you, Ray?" Buster asked me as he popped the cap off a Shiner Bock.

"I'm still considering my options," I told them. All three of the B's attacked at once, pouring their beer on my head. They knew my birthday of June 29th gave me a draft number of three-hundred-fifty-three, high enough that I was unlikely to get a greeting from Uncle Sam. Buster and I were born only a week apart, but that solitary week made all the difference in the Selective Service Administration lottery.

"Luck of the draw," Buster said, opening another cold one.

The day before graduation, I saw Buster standing stone cold still watching the custodian taking the flags down in front of our school. There was no ceremony, simply a routine part of the guy's close-of-business job. I never saw a boy look as full of himself as Buster, standing there with his hand over his heart while the American flag flapped around in the fading light as the custodian lowered it without a thought to protocol. When it reached the bottom, the janitor casually threw it over his shoulder along with the Lone Star Texas flag and trotted off inside, in a hurry to finish his shift and get home to his wife and kids. The custodian didn't see Buster, and I know neither of them saw me over by the gym.

Knowing how Buster's mind worked, I could imagine he had dreams of returning from the Army a hero on the battlefield with a chest full of medals. At that age none of us had given any consideration to why the USA was sending soldiers to fight in Indochina in the first place. Our World History teacher, who was also the basketball coach, tried to make a point about what he called the "domino effect," explaining that the big shots in Washington believed if one of the countries fell, the Commies would take the whole region. We made jokes since the only thing we knew about dominos was the game of Forty-Two.

That's how it is when you are eighteen. You think you'll always be able to run as fast as you want. Tomorrow you'll be even stronger than you were yesterday. If you stay out late, you sleep it off. You can eat what you want, when you want, and as much as you want. I remember when I could polish off two double cheeseburgers and fries for a snack and still eat three bowls of chili for supper with no heartburn. The boiler in my gut needed fuel because it was building the man I was becoming. I didn't have the sense God gave a billy goat to realize it was a passing state of being. Soon enough, I'd reach the top of the hill and then it was a long, slow slide down the other side. Hormones have a way of making you uncertain of whether the restless feeling in your jeans is patriotism or horniness.

Watching Buster's chest swell with pride as the janitor lowered those flags without fanfare made me want to have a piece of the action, too. Maybe that's what made me decide to join the Army Reserves. We never talked about it because Buster was packed up and gone a few days after graduation. So, he wound up in Vietnam, and I wound up a weekend warrior all because of a few days' difference in our birthdays. Luck of the draw. Him on one side of the bars. Me on the other. Him with a hole in his head and me still looking for answers.

* * *

Six active-duty pallbearers from Fort Hood placed Buster's flag-draped coffin on the bier with practiced precision and lined up to wait for the service to begin. The last person to arrive was Rev. Samuel Peter Thomas Burgess, or "Rev. B" to his radio parishioners. The last time I'd spent any real time with Rev. B was in connection with the Great Prayer Cloth Rip Off that landed a local mail carrier, Jackson Pruitt, in jail. Since I had a copy of Buster's will, I'd been expecting the Rev.

What I wasn't expecting was the way the old scoundrel was turned out. He was wearing a Class A uniform jacket from the

Vietnam era. To say he was wearing it is a bit of a misstatement. He'd likely had to commandeer some help to stuff his girth into the jacket. There was no way the front of that jacket could stretch over his ample paunch to permit a proper buttoning. He left it flapping open. You had to give him credit for making the effort. The proper uniform suit pants must have been a no-go since he'd opted for black store-bought knit trousers. His shirt and tie approximated regulation issue, but his Garrison cap sat perched atop his bushy mane as if a decoration or an afterthought.

The soldiers from Hood are taught to keep their eyes front and center and their expression neutral during this type of solemn duty assignment. But you've got to believe they were more than a little amused by the Rev's appearance.

Once the Rev took his place in front of the gathering, he uncovered his head and pulled some notes from the inside of the cap, smoothing them out and then making a show of taking out his reading glasses.

"Good afternoon ladies and gentlemen. I'm Reverend Samuel Peter Thomas Burgess. Some of you may know me from my on-air ministry. I met our friend there, Jonathan Francis McCombs," he said, with a sweeping motion to the coffin, "in the service. I was his chaplain."

Sara and Hattie looked at each other as if to say, "Who knew?" and Miss Lilly gave Ed's shoulder a comforting pat as Rev. B pushed on.

"Buster—we all knew him as 'Buster'—asked me to preach at his funeral. He told me straight up I'd better keep it short. I'll add, because we're all friends here, his language was a bit more colorful than the words I've just used." He looked out to the audience in expectation and was rewarded with a chuckle.

"I have a friend in the ministry who tells me what he likes about preaching funerals is carrying the Word to an audience that is honor bound by social convention and good manners to stay put once he starts. If you're not saved when he starts, he says, he just lays on enough fire and brimstone to be sure you are saved before he's finished."

At this point, Rev. B laughed out loud. He only got some serious seat-squirming in return. For all his faults, he could read a crowd, so he cut out the jokes and moved right into to talking about Buster.

"I was only with Buster's unit for a few weeks in Vietnam before I was reassigned. I had the pleasure of meeting some of his buddies. I remember one soldier from Idaho that he called 'Tater.' Another friend of his gave Buster the nickname 'Tex' for obvious reasons. I think his name was Samuel Singer. The three of them were inseparable.

"I hooked up with Buster again when I started my mission work here in Central Texas a few years back. By then he'd lost track of his Vietnam crew. It's a damn shame because I had the impression that they were like brothers over there. Buster was no longer the spit-and-polish, gung-ho private I'd met in country. The conflict shattered his nerves.

"Our Buster certainly didn't care about worldly possessions. He came from simple, home-grown stock and there never was any pretense about him. There's this question game I tried on the boys sometimes to get at what was important to them. I'd ask them to imagine their house was on fire and they only had time to save one thing as they ran to safety. What would that one thing be? The boys would usually change their minds several times or steal ideas from each other. Not Buster. He always came up with the same answer: his vacation pictures from his trip to Hawaii.

"I did promise Buster I'd keep it short. That's why, I suppose, I've said all I need to say. Buster was a soldier who did his duty and then came home. Lantz is the only place he ever wanted to be. His roots were here, and here's where he wanted to plant his bones. It was a boy who left Texas. It was a man who came back, carrying a heavy burden. Today, we can all rejoice and say he has finally laid his burden down. Can I get an 'Amen'?"

There was an awkward scattering of response and Rev. B moved on.

"Let us pray whatever he was looking for he will now find in that grace that only a loving God can give," Rev. said and then gave us all a hearty "Amen," to either teach us how it's done or to signal that the service was now over.

Right on cue *Taps* began to play. I could hear that familiar bugle mourn a thousand times and it would still send a chill through my nether regions every single time. You can almost sense a lone soul walking over the hill and turning one last time to wave goodbye as the sun goes down. Damn poetic if you ask me.

The Fort Hood soldiers began to remove and ceremoniously snap the casket flag into a tri-corner fold to present to Ed, him being the only family present. I got the impression he was taken by surprise when the army captain knelt in front of him and said those solemn words, dictated and standardized like almost everything else in the Army: "On behalf of the President of the United States, the United States Army, and a grateful nation, please accept this flag as a symbol of our appreciation for your loved one's honorable and faithful service."

Ed handed the flag off to Miss Lilly as if it was burning his hands. You could read on his face that his war, the one in Afghanistan, had just intruded on him and he needed to be somewhere else. He began to sweat and, for just a fraction of a second, I thought he was going to cut and run. Miss Lilly wrapped her arm around him and slipped her hand into his. Just as fast as it came on Ed, it passed, and the ceremony was over.

Miss Lilly stood and greeted folks as they moved in close to offer handshakes and hugs. There would be more of that later since my Sweet Wife was with some church ladies organizing a potluck at the General Store. Sara had closed for the afternoon and a few folks said they would drop by, in the way of small towns, to bury sorrow and offer good wishes over sheet cake and tuna salad.

Rev. B was telling Miss Lilly he'd be the first in line. That sounded about right to me. I would always consider him a charlatan who had hoodwinked a lot of good people, but on that day, he'd paid Buster his due.

A team from the cemetery would come to fetch Buster and put him in his hole, and that, as they say, would be that.

I, on the other hand, had more digging to do.

CHAPTER 32

There was a nice spread for the mourners at the General Store after services. For Ed's sake, I was glad to see a decent turnout of folks there to bid Buster a final glad-I-knew-you. I would have enjoyed my plate of food more if I hadn't been dreading the conversation I was about to have with Bobby. I'd given him time to consider his options and the FBI's proposal. Time was running out. I needed an answer and I needed it today. He was out back with R.W., Ed, and Miss Lilly when I caught up with him.

"R.W., have you tried the apple dump cake?" I asked. "It's going fast."

"Thanks for the tip," R.W. said. "Do believe I will. Can I bring anyone a piece?"

Everyone declined and he headed inside. I offered my condolences to Ed for the fifth or sixth time and reminded him I still had a few questions. Miss Lilly rewarded me with the stink eye, as expected, and suggested that Ed go inside with her to greet some of the guests.

"So, it's just the two of us," Bobby said with a nervous laugh after they left.

"We need to settle things."

"This is not the best place to have that kind of conversation."

"I agree. I'll meet you at the White House in half an hour. We need to get things wrapped up or the FBI will make their move."

"I know," he said, his eyes planted firmly on the toe of his boots. "I'll be there."

"Promise?"

"Promise."

* * *

I waited for Bobby on the patio that runs along the backside of the Arrowhead government building. Before my time, someone had cleared the brush and laid tile, hauled load at a time from trips to Ciudad Juárez and Nuevo Laredo. It was a mix of Saltillo twelve-inch squares and Talavera four-by-fours. Over time the surface had suffered with cracks where the seal wore away and weeds sometimes broke through the grout. Several of us who collect a government paycheck for a living make it our hobby to maintain the patio and surrounding woods as a private picnic area of sorts. It is one of the few perks of our jobs.

I'd sent Deputy Lake over to the wake to get something to eat. My daddy used to say some folks were as useless as tits on a turtle, and that pretty much describes what I think of Deputy Lake. Someday when things get back to what passes for normal around here, I'm going to make it my mission to figure out what he does with the time we pay him for.

With Johnnie out of the way, I opened the back window to make it possible to hear the phones if they rang. Then I settled into a comfortable chair and waited. I've always found the back patio was the best place if you wanted to have a decent conversation. The Sheriff's office with its holding cell, bulletin boards full of official notices, computers, and alarm system had a way making folks want to stop talking and ask for a lawyer. Get them in a comfortable chair under the open sky and their shoulders relax. Before you know it, they're telling you what's on their mind.

As I waited, I thought about Ed at the funeral and how much of Afghanistan he'd brought home with him. It was on that very patio that Ed and I had sat trading stories and enjoying a cold one about a year ago. He'd dropped by the office to check on his uncle, who was drying out in my holding cell. We'd watched the day fade and, given that there weren't any clouds to speak of, we were enjoying a first-class banquet of stars.

"Did I ever tell you about Dudley Brown who I served with?" Ed asked.

"Can't say I remember the name," I told him.

"He was from a village in Upstate New York called Manlius. When he was growing up, he dreamed about being an astronaut, but never qualified. On clear nights over there he'd point out the constellations in a way that made all the hell we were going through seem small and unimportant. He'd remind us that Voyager, the tiny spacecraft launched before we were born, was out there somewhere in interstellar space still doing its job."

"The Voyagers are the ones with the Golden Record," I said.

"That's right. Dudley said the record had Earth sounds like dogs and crickets and shit. What he appreciated was that it also had music, including Chuck Berry. Anyway, he said no matter what happened down here, the stars would go on and Voyager would keep on keeping on. We couldn't fuck up so much that we'd have an effect on the cosmos. Now the cosmos, on the other hand, could really fuck with us."

"Your friend sounds like a philosopher."

"He got into it so deep that he even hooked up with an online group that sent emails to the astrophysicists who made the decision to demote Pluto from a planet."

"What difference did it make?"

"Dudley said just because Pluto didn't look the same and was small and had an atypical orbit, a bunch of elites decided it didn't belong."

"Sounds like he took it personal."

"You got that right. On night patrol he'd fill us in about his latest exchange on the message boards and the petitions the various Plutonians were working on. Didn't like it if anyone disrespected the little guys. He was that kind of soldier."

"What happened to him?"

"Taliban got him."

I was put in mind of that conversation because often the people in investigations, like the people in wars, find themselves in places they don't belong. In Ed's story a sweet-tempered apple farmer with the heart of a stargazer wound up eating dust and shrapnel in an Afghan hellhole because politicians in Washington D.C. couldn't figure out an exit strategy for an endless war. In my case, a big-hearted cattleman with a taste for sour vegetables in spices and brine and a willingness to do a favor without asking a lot of questions waded into a political swamp and was sucked into the muck.

I heard Bobby Seville arrive and called to him to join me around back.

As he settled into his chair I said, "I'd offer you a cold one, but since this is official business we'd better not." I pointed to a candy jar I'd commandeered from Katie's desk. It was full of licorice jelly-beans and orange slices. "Help yourself."

"No thanks. I filled up at the potluck."

I poured some of the beans into my palm and after sucking on a couple, turned straight to business.

"What with the tapes and all, the FBI have you dead to rights, Bobby. Have you talked to a lawyer about all this?"

"Naw."

"Do you want to?"

"What do you think I should do?"

"I can't advise you on the law. However, if it were me, I wouldn't sign anything unless a lawyer looked it over first."

"Do you know somebody?"

"The firm Blake hired in Austin has a good reputation. Like I said though, I can't officially recommend anyone."

"How can I break it to R.W.?"

"Maybe they can find a way to seal it. Keep it secret."

"You think?"

"I doubt it. Most the time with family it's best to shoot straight. They usually find out anyway. Hate to sound like a broken record, but you should talk to a lawyer."

"I changed my mind. Think I'll take some of that candy," he said reaching for the jar.

While he had a mouth full of the sweet stuff seemed as good a time as any to introduce the bad news.

"R.W. lied for you. Told me you were home with him the night Miss Belle died."

"Why would he say that?"

"He either thought you killed Belle and needed an alibi. Or he needed an alibi for himself. We know at the time someone was strangling Miss Belle, you were in Austin being tape recorded by the FBI."

I heard the front door of the office open and close and R.W. call out.

"Come on back. We're on the patio," I yelled to him.

CHAPTER 33

R.W. walked out to the patio glancing from his daddy to me and back to his daddy. He had the kind of expression teenage boys get on their face when you give them the side-eye at breakfast the morning after they've been out late, drinking beer and driving recklessly. Their move is to play it under the radar until they can figure how much you know. You could almost see this calculus churning through R.W.'s mind.

"Johnnie Lake said you were expecting me."

"Sit down, son," Bobby said, his voice devoid of judgment.

R.W. pulled up a chair near us.

"The Sheriff here says you haven't been straight with him about what happened the night Miss Belle died," Bobby said. "It's time to stop the pussyfooting and set the record straight. Do you hear me?'

"Yes, sir."

"Before you say anything, I think you need to know a few things about me and what happened that night. I've told all of this to Ray. I need you to hear about it from me. I'm not proud of it, but if I'm asking you to be honest, then I need to set an example."

I have to hand it to Bobby. He didn't pull any punches. He started with the ashes and his fight with Belle. "Did you know about what Belle did with your mama's ashes?"

"Yes, sir. Everyone knew."

"How did that make you feel?"

"Honestly?"

"I would expect nothing less?"

R.W. didn't answer right away, just chewed on his bottom lip. When finally answered, he didn't make eye contact with either of us.

"Kinda mixed up. I know how much you loved Mama. I've tried to picture her and remember how she smelled and the sound of her voice. The memories won't come. She's always just been the smiling lady in the framed pictures . . . and that jar on the mantel. And, of course, in all those stories you tell."

Bobby couldn't mask the way his boy's comments affected him.

"Don't get me wrong," R.W. said with an earnest appeal to Bobby. "You know I love the stories."

"Don't try to kid an old kidder, son. When did you hear the story? Was it Belle?"

"Yes, sir. I know I shouldn't have laughed at the way she put one over on the preacher, but when Miss Belle told the story, I did. Then I thought about you and it kinda pissed me off since I knew how it would hurt you."

"So, you've known for a while."

"Yes, sir."

"Well, you're right about me being hurt. Belle and I had it out before I went to Austin."

"Don't say any more, Daddy. The Sheriff is setting you up."

"You let me worry about Ray. He knows everything I'm trying to tell you. Belle and I had words. It was not what you would call a particularly friendly exchange. She was alive when I left. Passed out drunk but breathing. I carried her upstairs and covered her up. Then I left."

"Alive? Are you sure?" R.W. got up and started pacing like he was confused and agitated. "Are you absolutely, one hundred percent sure?"

"Yes, I'm sure. As you know there were some knockout drugs in the mimosas she was drinking. It was strong stuff. It didn't kill Belle. It put her to sleep. That's why I thought she was drunk. Someone came in later and finished the job by strangling her to death. Right now, the finger points to Buster. Poor son of a bitch."

"You don't mean . . ." R.W. said with a gasp. "I thought the DPS arrested Blake Tackett."

I explained there was new evidence that appeared to clear Blake.

"I sure as hell didn't strangle her, either. Ray here can prove it. Can't you, Ray?"

"Yes, I can."

"Go ahead and tell him."

R.W. sat back down hard in his chair and grabbed the candy jar.

As I may have mentioned, R.W. is not one of those fellas who is given to listening. He's more of a talker. While I explained what the FBI folks were up to and how it gave his daddy an alibi, he didn't say a word as the full meaning of the consequences dawned on him. He sat there with the candy jar in one hand and the lid in the other.

"What do we do now, Daddy?"

"I tell you what you are going to do. You are going to explain why you lied to Ray and I am going to hire a lawyer to help me deal with the mess I've made."

"One of the problems I have, R.W., is the way we found Miss Belle, all tidy-like. Is there something you can tell us to help explain that?" I asked.

"I saw you leave," R.W. said to his father. "I wanted to surprise Miss Belle with some Stubb's. After I checked in at the Driskill, my plans fell through. I bought some ribs and brisket and drove back to Lantz. I thought she would be tickled."

"That's a lot of driving," I said.

"Not for me. I like the road. Helps me think."

He didn't have to explain the concept to me. I understood all about quietude, solitude, open roads and thinking.

"I thought we'd watch a movie and then I'd get back to A-town in time for some music on Sixth Street," R.W. said.

"Then what happened?" I asked.

R.W. explained that he was coming up the highway when he saw his daddy turn out of the Tackett driveway.

"I was coming from the other direction. I started to honk, but he was hightailing it. I figured I catch up with him back in Austin."

R.W. said the kitchen door was open and when he called Miss Belle didn't answer. He saw the sandwiches on the sideboard and glasses and pitcher. He kept calling to Miss Belle. When she didn't answer he went upstairs looking for her.

"She was laid out on her bed and looked gone. I thought, 'Oh my God,'" R.W. said, covering his eyes with both hands. "I was sure she was dead."

"And you thought I'd killed her?" Bobby asked.

"What was I to think? I tried to take her pulse and couldn't find it. I was scared."

He said he decided to try to make it look like she'd died in her sleep. He changed her into one of her frilly nightgowns and fresh bed slippers and tucked her into bed, pulling her sheet and bed-spread up around her shoulders.

"I even put Retinol cream on her hands and face the way she would have done herself. I wanted it would look right," he said. "I know that sounds creepy, but I thought I was protecting my daddy."

We didn't answer.

"What time did you leave?" I asked.

"I was there about an hour. I put a mimosa glass next to her bed so it would look like she had a drink before going to sleep. I tried to tidy up a bit before I left and I dumped the Stubb's in a trash can along the highway on the way back to Austin. I was a mess when I finally got there. I hooked up with some friends on Sixth Street and drank for a while."

"Anyone from the Cattlemen's meeting?" his daddy asked.

"No, sir. It was just some buddies. Guys from Austin and around."

"I'll need their names and contact information," I told him.

"Is that all?" he agreed, with a slight wince.

"Why didn't you come to me when they arrested Blake and straighten things out?" I asked.

His shoulders slumped and he looked at Bobby.

"I've wanted to do that every single day since you told us how Miss Belle really died. I was too afraid of disappointing my daddy."

CHAPTER 34

The next morning, I ignored the "Closed" sign on the door of the General Store. I could tell from all the trucks parked out front that everyone had gathered inside. I jiggled the knob and Sara opened the door.

"How you been?" I asked her.

"They're all here," she said, indicating I could come on in.

Ed McCombs, Miss Lilly, Blake Tackett, Bobby and R.W. Seville were crowded around their favorite table.

"Is there something we can do for you?" Miss Lilly asked.

"Wouldn't mind a cup of coffee," I answered.

"My pleasure," Sara said, fetching a mug. "Cream. No sugar."

I blew on the steaming cup and took a cautious sip. No one else moved or spoke. Papers that appeared to my untrained eye to be real estate plats were strewn across the table.

"Looks like you are working on something mighty important," I said, taking another sip of hot coffee.

"Is that an official inquiry or are you incredibly nosy?" Lilly responded, while the men looked on.

"I'd say maybe a mix of both," I offered with a scan of the people at the table, wondering if any of the others would break the ice. It was Ed McCombs who spoke up.

"Look everyone, Ray there is asking a simple question. No sense acting like it's some big secret."

"I've got work to do," Sara said, excusing herself. "Let me know if you need anything."

"It's like this, Ray," Ed said. "You remember that Uncle Buster was contacted by a pipeline company before he died. Seems they wanted an easement across his property. Planned to pay a nice sum. Problem is the line also needs to run across the Tackett and Seville places for it to be cost effective. The company was negotiating with all of us as well as several others around here," Ed said.

"I see," I answered. Truth be told I only half-assed understood. I figured if I kept quiet, they would unload. Blake did.

"I wanted to listen to the proposal. Belle dug her heels in. She said she didn't want an ugly pipeline spoiling her pasture. The truth is she had an unnatural fear of a leak or possibly an explosion. She was convinced gas lines were a fire hazard. Had this dream about the house going up in flames. It would wake her in the night and then she couldn't go back to sleep. I could argue till the cows come home but she'd made up her mind it wasn't safe and that was that. Bobby even talked to her. Ed talked to her. Hell, even Buster tried. She wouldn't budge."

"When did all this happen?" I asked.

Now it was Miss Lilly's turn.

"It's been a while. We all thought it was dead in the water and we'd forgotten about it. Then we got a call from the pipeline company," she said. "Seems they read about Mama's passing and wanted to talk. The project had been put on a back burner when the company had to downsize and reset priorities. Now the project is back on."

"So here we are," Bobby said.

"So here you are," I answered.

"That's not why you dropped by, though, is it, Ray?" Bobby said.

"No sir, it isn't. I've got a few questions for Blake when he has some time for me. It involves Sara, too."

I hadn't heard her come out of the back but suddenly realized that Sara was standing a ways off besides the counter. I didn't even try to decipher the expression that flashed between her and Blake.

"Is this about Belle?" Blake asked.

"And Buster. I'm still working a few loose ends. When can we talk?"

Bobby and R.W. stood up and started shuffling papers. "We can finish this later, Blake. There's a lot to think about."

Ed was the next to stand. "Need to get to work myself."

"I'll walk you out," Miss Lilly said.

Sara came over and started clearing the table. Blake grabbed her hand. "You don't need to do that."

"I know," she replied. "Helps me to stay busy."

I asked Sara to sit for a minute since what I needed to say, I needed to say to them both.

"Dadgummit, Sheriff, mighty early in the morning for you to be giving orders," she answered, but she stopped picked up cups and pulled up a chair.

I told them things were shaping up for the charges against Blake to be dropped. There was so much wire in his barn with his fingerprints on it that his Austin lawyer would make mincemeat of any attempt at prosecution. They had also done research on his so-called motive and confirmed that Miss Belle's life insurance listed Miss Lilly as the beneficiary, not Blake.

"I told them that," Blake said. "Both our policies were set up the same way."

"Just as important, it looks like they will tag Buster as the one who killed Miss Belle," I told them. "I've already told Ed."

"So that's it?"

"I still have one or two loose ends."

"Like what?" Sara asked.

"Like how the sedative got into the orange juice. I have some theories."

"Anything else?" Sara asked.

"One more thing. It's about the pineapple cake at the last church bake sale."

Sara gave me a shit-eating grin.

"I know how your mind works," I told Sara.

"You got me," she said, trying to hide a sheepish grin. "Mrs. Frierson didn't deserve what Belle said about her and it was all for a good cause. Blake is the one who ponied up the cash."

I polished off my coffee before heading to the door. It was just like Miss Belle to assume it was Bobby who taunted her by buying the cake instead of her husband. That's what set her off to telling folks about what she did on Ash Wednesday. Little acts with big consequences. No sense telling Sara and Blake.

* * *

I was twenty minutes early. The front door was unlocked and standing open. Inside, Sara's house looked dark and unnaturally quiet. I started to turn around and wait in my patrol car when I heard Mrs. Lawrence's soft cough.

"Hello, anyone home?" I asked the door.

"It's me, Sheriff. Come in if you want to."

It was easy to recognize the raspy voice of Sara's mama. A combination of years of heavy smoking and COPD had left her voice sounding like sixty-grit sandpaper being dragged over a cast iron skillet. I opened the door and looked in. At first, I had trouble locating Mrs. Lawrence in the dim room. Then she spoke again. She was standing at the hallway, holding tight onto her walker.

"Watch out for Twizy," she warned.

Too late. Hell Cat was on me before I cleared the threshold. She'd been hanging like a gargoyle on top of a bookcase by the front door. She left a four-inch scratch on my hand before skidding away.

"Hot damn. Son of a . . ." I stopped myself mid-cuss. Mrs. Lawrence is what you might call a strict constructionist when it comes to the Bible and adherence to the Word. It was Mrs. Lawrence who inspired the Great Pitch Pipe Schism at the Lantz Church of Christ. The Church, which as anyone can tell you who attends services with Campbellites, does not believe in using musical instruments for services. I will confess the congregation's full-throated *a cappella* singing does, for certain, honor the scripture's directive to raise up a joyful noise unto the Lord.

Anyhow, one day a new lay minister at Mrs. Lawrence's church brought a pitch pipe to Sunday morning services. He told them it would help everyone get on the same key. That's all it took. Things must have been going too good for too long and folks needed something to fuss about. Mrs. Lawrence demanded the ungodly instrument be thrown out. After a number of fractious meetings, prayers, and an all-out ruckus over the heresy imposed by the pitch pipe, a splinter group, led by Mrs. Lawrence, left the Lantz congregation, taking their tithes with them.

"Told you to watch out for the cat. I'm going back to my room. You can come if you want," Mrs. Lawrence said. Without waiting for a response, she began the arduous work of turning around, step by careful step.

It was slow going. Mrs. Lawrence slid the aluminum frame forward a few inches and then walked each foot into the safety zone before sliding the rack forward again. I followed behind, ready to catch her if she lost her footing. It wasn't necessary. She was well-practiced in the walker shuffle and eventually made it to the rocker-recliner in her bedroom. The slow turn necessary to position herself over the chair seemed to exhaust her because she dropped into the seat with a soundless sigh as if there was insufficient air in her lungs to produce noise.

The chair swallowed up her tiny bones into a dent in the fabric, worn there by months of sitting and waiting for the end. I pulled up a straight-back chair near her and watched while she struggled to adjust a crocheted throw over her scrawny knees. I knew better than to insult her by attempting to help.

"I'd like to apologize to you, Mrs. Lawrence, for my rough language when I arrived."

She was having none of it.

"Now, Ray, you know it's not me you need to be asking forgiveness for such talk. It's the Good Lord's forgiveness you must seek."

"Yes, ma'am."

"I know your mama never allowed you to blaspheme in her house," she said. "She was a good woman. Never forget that."

"Yes, ma'am."

I think she would have chewed me out more if she hadn't started to cough so hard, I was scared she might choke.

She grabbed a handful of Kleenex and I tried to look away when she spit out a what looked to me like a piece of bloody lung. She pointed to the water pitcher. I filled a glass for her and held it steady while she took a few sips. It was a while before her breathing returned to normal, or what passed for normal for her.

"We're both a bit bloody today," she said pointing to the deep cat scratch on my hand. "There's some ointment and Band-Aids in the bathroom. Better go take care of your wound, Sheriff."

I excused myself and cleaned up in the bathroom down the hall. When I returned, she was holding the water glass in both hands. They were trembling so bad she couldn't get the glass to her mouth. I helped her again. I sat the glass back down and waited. That's when she made a statement out of left field.

"Let's get one thing straight. I didn't vote for you."

"No, ma'am."

She took another long, rattling breath. "Have you figured it out?"

"Pretty near."

"Took you long enough."

"You didn't make it easy."

She tried to laugh. Instead, she produced another round of wheezing and coughing. We did the tissue-water-sipping routine again, and she laid back in the recliner and pulled the flimsy throw up around her shoulders.

"I guess I'm about done in," she said in a voice so low I could barely make out her words.

"Yes, ma'am."

"Do you have a tape recorder with you, Sheriff?"

"There's one in the car."

"You'd better get it. I may not be able to tell this story more than once."

When I came back and turned on the recorder, I asked her if she wanted to call a lawyer. I ran through her rights against self-incrimination and such. She cackled.

"You and I both know I won't live long enough to go to jail or stand trial. Let's get this going," she said, pointing to turn the tape. "It's been a long time coming."

After I started the recorder and explained in official language the when and where of what was going on, she told her story.

She said she first got the idea of killing Belle in her head when Sara was in high school.

"There's an old expression up in the East Texas piney woods where I was raised," she said. "Some people, folks say, need killing. Belle Tackett was one of them. As a Christian woman, I fought the impulse as long as I could."

She pointed to the cross-stitch sampler hanging over her disheveled bed. It read simply: "Romans 12:19."

"'Vengeance is Mine; I will repay, saith the Lord,'" I quoted.

"I see you know your scripture, Sheriff. Your mama raised you right."

"I have reason to be familiar with that particular passage, yes, ma'am."

"It's important to keep up with your Bible studies. Every night when I say my prayers, I look at that cross-stitch and I pray extra hard for the Good Lord to give me the strength to fight the urge that was put in me all those years ago when Sara was in high school. I've asked for the strength not to seek vengeance on Belle. In the end, I was too weak."

"What happened when Sara was in high school?"

Mrs. Lawrence's story started to wander like she didn't hear the question. I wondered, not for the first time, if all this would ultimately turn out to be the babbling of a senile old woman close to death rather than a murder confession. She talked about how she'd felt guilty when she had to farm out her children to different family members after her husband died. It was the only way she could manage to move to Dallas and finish schooling as a Licensed Vocational Nurse. When she got back to Lantz, the only place she could afford was a run-down apartment at Cross Timbers Courts on the highway.

"It was a mosquito-infested nightmare of a place. The plumbing barely worked and we had no air conditioning," she said. "In the summer, the kids would soak washcloths and put them in the freezer, then lay them over their bodies and stretch out in front of our sad little oscillating floor fan to try to cool down."

Mrs. Lawrence stopped talking and closed her eyes. I was afraid she'd dozed off. Then she opened her eyes. They were old lady eyes like smokey glass that had faded out in places where bits of sand had stuck to them. She looked straight at me although I wasn't sure she could even see me because her eyes didn't seem to be in focus.

"At least my family was under one roof. That's all that counts in the end."

She closed her eyes again and kept up her story.

"One day Sara came home all excited because a friend was coming for a sleep over. I decided I would do my best to prepare a supper fit for company. I camouflaged a can of Spam with a jelly glaze. It could almost, just almost, pass for baked ham, if you didn't look too close. I even put some parsley in with the boiled potatoes and bought an extra can of fruit cocktail. I was proud to make the effort for Sara, even though I knew it was a poor man's dinner."

When it came time for her friend to arrive, the car drove up to the curb out front. Her friend didn't get out. Sara came back inside crying. Her friend told her that her parents wouldn't allow her to stay at the Courts because it wasn't safe. She may have used the phrase "white trash." Her so-called friend was Belle.

"I knew it was all a set-up. My child's heart was broken. I let her cry for a while and then I told her enough was enough. I dragged her off the bed and splashed her face with a glass of iced water. Then I sat her down at the table. No sense wasting a perfectly good can of Spam."

Mrs. Lawrence was talking faster now, as if the memory was tapping into a reserve of forgotten adrenaline.

"After supper I gave her a good talking to. We don't let other people tell us who we are. We decide who we are. They may think we are cousin-marrying-trailer-trash-Bible-thumpers without enough sense to come in out of the rain. They can say what they want. It don't matter. We get to say who we are and what we believe."

Mrs. Lawrence started coughing again and I thought this time she was going to pass for sure. Her skin color changed from gray to a blue tinge, and she couldn't seem to catch her breath. I turned off the tape recorder and got out my cell phone, thinking I would call for an ambulance. She slapped the phone out of my hand. After a while, her breath returned to its regular rasping sound and with a few more sips of water she motioned me to turn the tape back on.

"Let's get this done," she said, with more conviction than I would have thought possible under the circumstances.

I explained the interruption into the recorder and Mrs. Lawrence picked up her story where she left off.

"Sara never forgot that night. Neither did I. Maybe I could have looked the other way and let bygones be bygones if Belle hadn't kept after Sara."

"Forgive me for saying so, Mrs. Lawrence. This all seems like old news. Why now? Why take her life now?"

"Ain't it obvious?"

She pointed to the bloody tissues in the trashcan.

"I've run out of time. My boys aren't worth the salt on their popcorn. Sara is the only one who's taken care of me. Belle was in the way of her happiness and it was up to me to do something. I saved up my medicine and rode along with Sara when she dropped those sandwiches off. Told her I wanted to see the inside of Belle's house one more time. Sara didn't have a clue. I dumped the whole kit and caboodle in that pitcher. Done it for my Sara."

Mrs. Lawrence started shaking and rattling in her chest like a coughing fit was about to start up again, so I waited.

"Now you go on and do what you need to do, Ray Crawford, and leave me be," she mumbled.

"Do you need anything before I go?"

"The Good Book, if it's not too much trouble," she said pointing to a New Testament with a cracked black cover and faded gold lettering on the table. Her hands were curled up, clutching Kleenex so I just laid her Bible gingerly within reach. She reached out and wrapped one hand around the text pulling it to her bosom the way a child might cuddle a favorite stuffed doll at bedtime, comforted by the security of the familiar.

I figured there wasn't anything left to say. I picked up the tape recorder, collected my hat, and left quietly, closing the door behind me.

CHAPTER 35

The road home from Austin seemed longer than usual. My mind wandered, replaying my conversation with Phil at the DPS where I'd gone to close the case of Miss Belle's murder.

"The story started when Bobby Seville first heard about what Belle had done with his Monica's ashes," I told Phil.

That's why he left the note for her and why he went over to see her. Of course, Hattie Mae knew it was Bobby Seville who was expected because of the Depression glass all laid out in the dining room, and it was Hattie who saw Sara dropping off the sandwiches and ice cream. What she didn't see was Grace Lawrence in the front seat, because the little old lady's forehead barely cleared the bottom of the window.

Bobby Seville admitted he was hot under the collar and exchanged words with Miss Belle. She was alive when he helped her up to her room, nearly passed out from what he assumed was one too many mimosas. R.W. showed up with barbecue at the same time his daddy drove away. When he couldn't feel a pulse, he was scared shitless his daddy had killed Miss Belle in a fit of anger about the ashes. In a misplaced attempt to protect good ol' Bobby,

R.W. did what he could to try to make it look like Belle had died in her sleep. He didn't do a very good job because in his haste he overlooked what was lurking in the bottom of the mimosa pitcher.

Later, after Blake Tackett returned early from Austin, he and Buster McCombs got into a knock-down-drag-out fight at Sara's place. It turned ugly and violent because Buster had been drinking all day. After Buster left Sara's in a blind alcoholic rage, he went to Miss Belle's. When he found her passed out, he strangled her with a piece of wire he found in Blake's shed.

Phil pulled up a file on his computer and hit the print button.

"That's the medical examiner's semi-final report on Mrs. Tackett," he said. "Looks like the wire may have been window dressing. He could have just as easily suffocated her simply by covering her nose and mouth since she was in no shape to put up a struggle. The wire was possibly there to incriminate her husband. Almost worked."

"Trouble is Buster was given to forgetfulness and blackouts when he got drunk," I said. "I can't be certain he even remembered killing Miss Belle until later. I think it's possible at some point after I talked to him, the memory caught up with him."

Phil printed a second report. This one was the findings from the autopsy on Buster.

"Gunshot to the head. We're ruling that it was self-inflicted," he said, handing the printout to me for my file. "A troubled man with a troubled past."

"What happened to him in combat ate him alive for the rest of his life."

"Seems so."

"Did you find out anything about the Colt?" I asked.

"Looks like a dead end," Phil said. "There are enough damn loopholes in gun registration laws that we may never trace it. If we do, I'll let you know."

Phil pulled out the same yellow notepad he'd used when we met at the start of the case and began flipping through the pages, marking here and there with a Sharpie. "From what I have here, we started this investigation with seven suspects. Seven solid citizens, each with a reason to kill your Mrs. Tackett. You say you've cleared them all except the one who is no longer alive. Am I getting that right, Ray?"

"That's right. Blake and Sara were together. Ed and Miss Lilly give each other an airtight alibi, and they can place R.W. in Austin at the time of death. He gave me the name of friends who corroborate his alibi.

"What about your Mr. Seville?" Phil said.

I squirmed in my seat since I wasn't certain how far I could go with the FBI top secret, undercover information. Then Phil burst out laughing and gave me that damn Texas Tech guns up shit.

"You can relax Ray. Max called and gave me the lay of the land on Bobby's little escapade."

I was so relieved I didn't even mind that Phil had played me.

"With that FBI situation, Bobby's now off of our list of suspects," I said.

"No loose ends? All seven original suspects accounted for," he said.

"We did have one surprise," I told him, summarizing the conversation with Grace Lawrence, and providing a duplicate of my interview tape.

"That's some serious small town revenge you have going on in Lantz," Phil said when I finally came up for air.

"Little acts with big consequences," I agreed.

"What are you going to do about her?"

"Nothing."

"Attempted murder?"

"Hospice says Mrs. Lawrence's got, at most, a week left on this good earth. She thinks she avenged her daughter. Let her die thinking that. I may as well leave it to the Good Lord to sort out the actual sins from the nefarious intentions."

"Can't rightly say I disagree."

"Appreciate that."

"Hell of a story. All tied up in a neat ribbon."

"Yep."

"No one to charge. No one to arrest."

"Nope."

"Hell of a deal."

"So you said."

Phil asked for some bureaucratic-type paperwork and told him I would be happy to oblige. He suggested we grab something to eat at Threadgill's. It was a tempting offer, but I lied, telling him my Sweet Wife was expecting me.

I'd kept a few details of the story to myself and was feeling a bit shameful for it. The story about the pineapple cake, for instance. Seemed it didn't add a lot, but I figured it was what set Miss Belle to telling her story about Monica's ashes. She'd got it in her head that Bobby was the one who bought the overpriced cake just to spite her, and she was vindictive enough to try to hurt him.

Then there was the business about the receipt from the Conoco gas station in Florence. The time stamp put Buster there around seven. It didn't mean he couldn't still get to Belle's house in time to smother her. Establishing exact time of death is a soft number at best but it bothered me. Loose ends always do.

I suppose worrying over loose ends is part of what added miles to the trip back to Lantz and sorting out what I owed to the DPS and what I owed to the people of Lantz. My mind was not on the road as I eased around the familiar curves on the drive home when my police radio lit up and Katie Sue's voice crackled through.

"Sheriff, what is your 10-20?"

"I'm about fifteen minutes out, Katie. What's up?"

"We've got us a great big ol' 10-70."

Before I could ask for a translation, she obliged.

"It's the Tackett place. It's on fire."

* * *

That was one of the longest days I can remember in my career as Sheriff. I smelled the fire before I saw it. The heat was so fierce you couldn't pull a clean breath. Half of Lantz turned out. Most of the men in Arrowhead County are volunteer firemen. The rest in the crowd were rubberneckers. Our local Volunteer Fire Department is enthusiastic but not particularly efficient or well-equipped. The problem was that after two years of near drought, there wasn't enough water pressure to fight a blaze the size of that one.

By midnight, the boys and I were pretty much covered in soot and fully spent. We had to concede that the devil was going to have his way. We settled down across the road to watch the place burn into the night, all of Miss Belle's tchotchkes and pseudo-antiques turning into a pile of rubble and charcoal.

The State Fire Marshal did a fine job of investigating and concluded the problem was faulty electrical wiring. I'm not one to question the expertise of the Marshal's folks. But I can't help but wonder if Miss Belle's premonitions about fires and her fears had come to something.

After Sara buried her mother, she and Blake bought an Airstream and took to the road. The choices people make don't often surprise me, but I did get a kick out of the thought of Blake, who'd never before even left Texas, all of a sudden waking up to a new stretch of road every morning. Then there was Sara, back in a trailer, happily shed of all that had tied her down for her entire life. They made it a point to check in from time to time.

It was most unfortunate that Hell Cat wasn't a welcome traveling companion for the pair. That's how Twizy, that cross between a worn-out wool blanket and an annoying chin hair you miss when you're shaving, came to live at the police station. It was Katie Sue Brooks and my Sweet Wife who insisted. I had an eyeball-to-eyeball with the beast until we finally made an agreement about how things were going to work. I'll be damned if Hell Cat didn't seem to understand every word I said. When push came to shove, Twizy turned out to be the best deputy I ever had. One snarl from that monster and drunks sobered up and con men got religion.

Ed and Miss Lilly cleared the debris left when the old Tackett Victorian burned to the ground and built an architectural wonder in its place. It's made of native stone and pecan wood with vaulted ceilings and enormous windows that welcome daylight and moon glow. They had three kids, all brats who talk sass but are smart as whips.

Across the road, they hauled off all of Buster's trash and that sorry excuse for a house trailer. They took down that pitiful fence and left an open field that attracts bees, butterflies, and birds. Each spring the meadow turns into a thing of natural beauty filled with mounds of native wildflowers, and folks pull off the road to take pictures of their kids and even their dogs sitting in blankets of Texas bluebonnets.

The General Store remains the center of everything and now sports one of those impressive Texas Historical Commission markers. You can tell someone from Austin wrote what's on the plaque because it reads like an obituary, or a resume, since the text is chock-full of dates and names. This, of course, completely misses the living, breathing soul of the place. The life that soaked into the spine of the place. Words on a plaque can't capture the tragedy of almost-but-not-quite elegant moments tucked between decades of humdrum. It can't tell you about the greed, lies, heartbreaks, hopes, and passion. It misses the hanging-on-by-your-fingertips survival through tough times and, in the end, death. Who we are, who we became, who we should be, all worked out as the seconds and minutes and hours tick by. The decades dripping through time, seeping into the timber and the floorboards of a place like the Store. You can't put that on a plaque.

Speaking of plaques, Katie Sue Brooks finally got one from her old high school. I think I mentioned that she's a natural whiz with spreadsheets and computers. Well, long story short, she was at a training session sponsored by the DPS when she met up with a young programmer. Turns out her young fella was on assignment as part his corporation doing outreach to help solve government data bottlenecks or some such. Katie and the programmer wound up sitting next to each other at the conference. Katie being Katie, she talked his fool head off about Lantz and Arrowhead County and how she'd set up accounting and case files on Excel spread-sheets. The guy was one of your classic nerds, writing down everything she said. They went to lunch and Katie kept talking.

The next day when he was giving his talk, the corporate nerd mentioned Katie's ideas and before long they were collaborating on an application that, I kid you not, was later used by most of the smaller law enforcement departments across the state. Seems one of the keys to the success of the program was setting it up with menus and screens that use terminology and icons familiar to cops in their daily routine. Puts me in mind of the little trashcan that was popular on early Apple computers back in the day. All that time Katie spent learning police code talk finally paid off. Of course, it's more complicated than a few cute, cop-friendly icons. Behind the screen, out of sight, algorithms, whatever they are, talk to state databases in new and unprecedented ways.

The big bosses at corporate were so happy with the way the project turned out they gave a grant to our local high school to fund a computer lab. The school named it for our very own Katie Sue. The lab has a plaque on the wall and everything. Katie Sue and her programmer friend have been keeping company, so I think that part worked out, too.

Bobby and my Sweet Wife started a business they called *Pickled Everything* just in time for the charcuterie craze. They couldn't produce the stuff fast enough to meet the demand for brined vegetables to pair with high-priced deli meats and farm-to-table cheeses. Fancy restaurants, gourmet food shops, and catered parties couldn't get enough of their product. They made a ton of money. Their concoctions were featured in articles in both *Texas Monthly* and *Southern Living*. Needless to say, my buttons were popping with pride to see S.W. in her element.

It breaks my heart that Bobby didn't live long enough to enjoy it. He and R.W. finally took Monica's ashes to Maryland. I gave them a lift to the Austin airport and we had time to chew the fat a bit before the flight. He was in a melancholy mood because they wouldn't let him carry the urn on the plane with him. You could see the pull as he checked the bag. It was the first time the urn had been out of his possession.

R.W. left us at the snack bar while he went off to buy a paperback to read on the flight. Bobby kept glancing over his shoulder at the airline check-in where passenger luggage was tumbling down a conveyer belt. I could practically read his mind.

"It'll be all right," I told him with more confidence than I felt.

"I don't know what I'll do without her," he said. "Sometimes when I first wake up, when my bones are still paralyzed after a nap, I feel Monica in the house. It's a sense that I'm not alone, that she's in the other room, and that I should go check on her to make sure she's okay. I never get to the point where I act on it. It's sometimes a faint mist or a half dream. A feeling more than a thought. I know she doesn't belong on a shelf. It's not what she wanted, but I don't know what I'll do if I lose her again."

The boys stayed over in Maryland to spend time with Monica's relatives. R.W. returned ahead of time, but Bobby said he wanted to spend another week to visit a few more of Monica's favorite places. He was on his way to the airport for the return trip to Texas when his rent car slid off a slick mountain road in bad weather. He didn't survive the crash. R.W. had Bobby cremated and his ashes joined Monica's. Several of us flew up for the services. Not a one of us apologized for the tears we shed. That fine fella never did have to testify against the Cattlemen after all.

CHAPTER 36

Just under two decades slipped by before I held the Tackett case file in my hands again. I hauled the box containing the file and exhibits off the top shelf of the storage room and eased it slowly down to Katie.

"Careful of the dust," I warned, a bit late, as she let out a head-snapping sneeze and nearly dropped the box.

After twenty-plus years as Sheriff, it was time to retire. Before packing it all in, I was working with Katie, who had arranged for closed case files to be digitized. Fancy word that. Bless her heart; she'd always managed to keep us one step ahead of becoming obsolete.

Opening that storage box was like taking hold of an old bone you dig out of the yard, dry and cracked and shaped like memories you'd as soon as not forget.

We'd spread out the paperwork and photos on my desk when my former deputy Johnnie Lake breezed in. Or should I say Mayor Lake. How a good-for-nothing, lazy-ass man like Johnnie Lake managed to get elected Lantz Mayor three terms in a row beats the hell out of me. That's politics for you.

"What you folks up to?" he asked, as if it wasn't apparent.

Katie told him what we were doing and offered him something cold to drink.

While she fetched him a Dr Pepper, he pulled up a chair and began messing around with the open file until he came across copies of the paperwork from the company that wanted an easement across Buster's place.

"Heart of Texas Pipeline Company. They sure used to have one ugly logo now, didn't they? Big tacky red heart. H.O.T. with orange flames. You'd think with all that money they could afford something nice," he said, pointing to the letterhead on the maps. "It was painted on all their trucks back in the day. That's why I could spot it from a distance."

Now on a regular day, I wouldn't pay much attention to Johnnie because what he says means damn little. But in this case, the way he said that last bit made me want to scratch an old itch.

"How far away were you when you spotted the trucks?"

Johnnie gave me one of his sheepish grins that wasn't charming when he was a young man and sure as hell didn't work now that he had ruts on his face and a beer belly. I waited until he'd uncapped his Dr Pepper and taken a swig to give him time to contemplate.

"Suppose it don't matter anymore but I used to visit my cousin who worked for the electrical co-op. They have those lift baskets to work on the lines. If the weather is good, you can see all around for sixty miles or more. It's better than an amusement ride at Six Flags. Sometimes he and his buddies would let me go up and hang out. I could see all of Lantz and the roads around. Very, very cool."

"Did you see anything interesting?"

"Sure did."

"Such as?"

"For one thing, R.W. leaving the Tackett place on Miss Belle's last day. That was before the H.O.T. truck pulled up. Guess the H.O.T. folks wanted to talk to Blake about the pipeline. Too bad he left for Austin early," he said with a shrug, working on his soda.

I could feel the caps on my molars grating against one another. I tried to take time to measure out my next question.

"Seems this is something you might of mentioned before now."

"Didn't want to get my cousin in trouble. Might have lost his job. Besides, what difference did it make? You figured out who done it, right? Old Buster was the one who killed her. Too bad he wasn't alive when the H.O.T. truck came to see him about the pipeline. Might have given him a reason to live, too."

"Say again."

"Saw them at his trailer that morning. I guess he'd already shot himself by then."

When I was younger, I might have had the patience to sit there and chew a bit on what he'd served up. I was too old and too ornery since my Sweet Wife died to give a rat's tail anymore.

"Johnnie Lake, you are one sorry excuse for a human being," I said. "Unless you have city business, I would appreciate it if you would take your soda and get your useless carcass out of my office."

"You can't talk to me that way, Sheriff," he said.

"Just did," I replied, pointing to the door.

He grabbed his hat and left, attempting to slam the storm door for a dramatic effect. What with the pneumatic door closer, it oozed shut so that he managed to look like the fool he was. I made a beeline for the patio out back as it was still the only place where I could think. I was stove up from climbing the ladder in the storage room and what with arthritis in one knee and titanium in the other, my exit wasn't so much of a storm-out-of-the-room as a

238 · D.L.S. EVATT

hobble-out-of-the-room. Forgive me for injecting my medical condition into this story. I don't like to think I've turned into a hypochondriac in my golden years, but I do find myself talking about my health with greater regularity.

I had no sooner settled my bones into a chair when my phone pinged, telling me I had a text message from Sara. She said she and Blake had left their pickup and Airstream in a little town near Seattle and caught the Alaska State Ferry to Juneau. Attached was a picture of Blake. He'd grown a gray beard and was leaning on the ferry's railing, staring at a pristine coastline of rocky cliffs that shoved their way into a choppy ocean, the wind tossing his shoulder length white hair every which way. In her text, Sara said Blake wanted me to know he'd figured out the answer. He said I would understand.

It chaps my ass to admit it, but Johnnie had a point. What difference did anything make now? It helps if you finally know the truth because then you can put down your spade and quit digging. Like the folks out at the Gault archeological site who discovered the people who lived in these parts all those centuries ago. They kept excavating until there were no more layers of truth to find. They didn't stop until they knew all there was to know. That's when they put down their tools, quit digging, and filled in the hole. Seems that's what I needed to do now that I had hit bedrock.

Since I started writing up this tale, a lot of ideas have wiggled out of my memories. I put it all down, hoping it would help. Some of it feels only half remembered. I tried to be true to the story, as I recall the truth. I suppose it takes a certain bit of brass to think you can tell how other people lived and how they felt and why they did what they did. I included what I knew of their hearts and their history. Where they came from and who they became. There is no way to tell it all because there is no way I could know it all.

I do know this to be true. A big part of who we are comes from how we were raised, our mamas and papas, our grandparents and aunts and uncles, so I included that where I remembered it. Part of who we are comes from the friends we have, the choices we make, and the choices made for us. I tried to include what I knew of that, too. I gave it a shot. I owed it to them. I owed it to Bobby and I owed it to Belle and, mostly, I owed it to Buster. Truth be told.

I've put this story, as I've come to write it down, in the closed case file and now I'll seal it away. I'm not sure anyone will ever read a file like this from a backwater Texas town where a couple of folks with a lifelong vendetta got in the way of a big gas company's greed and the local sheriff was too stupid or too much of a hayseed to see the truth. I can only hope if someday some sorry sumbitch who has the misfortune to pin on a badge in Arrowhead County dusts off this lost tale, the lessons I tell here will come in handy.

In school we're taught this country of ours is founded on the principle that all men are created equal and endowed with unalienable rights given to all by the creator, those rights being: life, liberty, and the pursuit of happiness. After what I've learned from my years as Arrowhead Sheriff and from the deaths of Miss Belle and Buster, on most days the pursuit of happiness seems like a tall order. It's enough most days just to be able to dodge misery.

The last thing I'll do when I close the lid on this file is take down that hand-painted Latin sign left over from the previous occupant of this office and stick it in the box. Dura lex, sed lex. The law is harsh but it's the law. It's a fine sentiment in textbooks and Hollywood movies, but this is Arrowhead County, Texas, where it turns out law enforcement and the law can sometimes be upside-down.

At the end of the day I suppose all you can hope to do is dig until you uncover all the truth that's there. Sometimes you can enforce the law and sometimes you can seek justice, but you shouldn't ought to fool yourself into thinking they are the same thing.

ACKNOWLEDGMENTS

After my mother came to stay with me in her final years, I would drive her home on weekends so she could water her flowers and visit family. Our favorite route took us through rural backroads from Austin to Killeen. For entertainment, I would make up stories about the people who lived in the houses we passed along the way, using things I saw in their yards or the way they maintained their place as prompts to construct wild fantasy tales about the lives and personalities of the imaginary residents. She encouraged me then, as she did throughout my life, to write down my stories. No doubt the seed of this book was planted on those car trips. That's why my first acknowledgment belongs to my mama, Charlotte Shipp.

The storytellers in my life are many and remain a rich source of inspiration. They've shared memories—humorous, scary, poignant—that I adapted in the telling of this tale. For their generosity and cleverness and willingness to let me put a piece of their stories in this book, I will be forever grateful. My heartfelt thanks belong especially to Elva and Darla Schultz, Joann Howard, Kathy

McMaster, Rhonda Willard, Susan Galbreath, Chevis R. Cleveland, Kathy Thatcher, and Johnnie DeMoss.

I want to give a special shout out to my friend and partner in crime, Betty Cosgrove, whose stories about and pictures of her real-life Twizy, an irascible Maine Coon, were the inspiration for the antics of Hell Cat in these pages.

When it came time to sit down and write, I needed a retreat and found one in Dripping Springs. Helen Currie Foster and her husband, Larry, opened the doors of Casa Burro, a sanctuary tucked away near their home where the only disturbance was a daily visit from the resident burros. There I was able to sort through piles of random bits of writing that I'd accumulated and give shape to this mystery. Over glasses of wine and rye whiskey on cool evenings, we concluded that a true genre for mysteries set in small Texas towns, not unlike the classic English village mystery, was coming of age under the Lone Star's big sky. Helen's Alice MacDonald Greer mystery series fits this genre, and I can only hope that *Bloodlines & Fencelines* will rest comfortably on the bookshelf next to them.

Research can trip up any writing project. In my work for this book I got lucky because I was able to call on trusted resources. I can't name them all here but want to mention Mikeal Clayton, David Palmisano, Brenda Buck, and Crispin Ruiz for sharing their personal expertise. I was also aided by the Texas A&M University publication "The Five Strands: A Landowner's Guide to Fence Law in Texas"; David Ciambrone's book *Poisons: The Handbook for Writers*; and advice by Luci Hansson Zahray and her lecture on poisons at the Bouchercon 2019 conference in Dallas. I also owe thanks to the generous staff of the Texas Health and Human Services Commission who opened the gates of the Austin State Hospital cemetery for a tour of the facility and who patiently answered my questions. Those who know this sacred ground will recognize that my labeling of the stone markers does not comport with the numbering style used at the cemetery. This was intentional. Out of respect, I did not want to risk inadvertently choosing the number of an existing grave marker.

While writing this book I drew support from a strong community of local writers who gave me their time and encouragement, including friends and colleagues who read first drafts and offered insightful critique. Among these were Crispin Ruiz, Helen Foster, Mikki Daughtry, Grace Bradshaw, Kathy Waller, and Rodney Sprott.

I also drew support from one of Austin's most reliable sources of creative energy, all of the weekly congregants of Artist's Way lead by the indomitable Ann Ciccolella, Artistic Director for Austin Shakespeare. Among the congregants is the multi-talented Diana Borden, a masterful photographer. When I asked if she would allow me to use one of her pastoral scenes for my book cover, she decided to go on a photo shoot along the country roads around Central Texas. She returned with a collection of two-lane roads, fences, store fronts, fields, and horizons for me. I wanted them all but ultimately settled on the fenceline that graces the cover.

I would be remiss if I didn't also acknowledge the contribution of members of my mystery book reading group, Tuesdays Are To Die For. We've met monthly for many years to dissect the mystery books we've read. These lovers of the genre have taught me some of the most important lessons any writer can learn. After all, the ultimate audience for any book is the reader. Thank you each for your valuable insights, likes, dislikes, and wisdom.

Finally, although my story is told through the voice of a man, I like to think that at its core it is the story of women, especially mothers, wives, aunts, sisters, and grandmothers. Women who raise children and grieve for lost ones. Good women, wicked women, complex women, foolish and petty women, strong women, silly women. Independent, resilient, fearless, no-bullshit women. Competent women who never forget your birthday, who can assemble a delicious supper from leftovers and canned meat, and who can coax miraculous gardens from dry, spent soil. Women with that sixth sense to call, out of the blue, when you are down in the dumps. Women who get up every morning, pull on support hose over varicose veins, and go to work with little expec- tation that today will be any better than yesterday yet still teach their children to aspire, to do right, to dream. My last and most heartfelt acknowledgement I've saved for all those women I've known who inspired the characters in this book. I hope I did you proud.

If you like mysteries, try these by Meredith Lee:

Shrouded: A Crispin Leads Mystery
Insecure American graduate student Crispin Leads comes to the Vatican to study burial rituals and catch up with her oldest friend, Sister Lew, historian for the Shroud of Turin. Within hours of Crispin's arrival she witnesses a murder and is drawn into an investigation of multiple homicides.

Digging Up the Dead: A Crispin Leads Mystery
This adventure finds our young scholar dodging murderers and outwitting con artists on three continents as she tracks down the truth about the fabled Curse of King Tut's Tomb, modern killers, and horrific family secrets. Crispin must match wits with dark forces and battle personal demons if she is to dig up the long-buried truth. Move over King Tut.

Learn more about these stories at: www.meredithlee.net

One more thing before you go . . . .

Thank you for reading *Bloodlines & Fencelines*. There are plenty of books to choose from, so I'm proud that you chose this one. If you have time to post a review on Amazon, it can make a difference in sales, so that's nice, too. If you have comments or questions for me, I'd like to hear from you. You can send me a note by going to my website: www.dlsevatt.com

CPSIA information can be obtained
at www.ICGtesting.com
Printed in the USA
FSHW022035031121
85893FS